T0316531

Soldier's Wife

Pat Wambui Ngurukie

moran
PUBLISHERS

Moran (E. A.) Publishers Limited,
Judda Complex, Prof. Wangari Maathai Road,
P. O. Box 30797, Nairobi.

With offices and representatives in: Uganda, Rwanda, Tanzania, Malawi and Zambia

www.moranpublishers.com

First published 1989 by Macmillan Press Limited
This edition is published by Moran (E. A.) Publishers Limited 2013

ISBN 978 9966 63 232 6

2016		2015		2014		2013	
8	7	6	5	4	3	2	1

Acknowledgement

For me, writing is a gift from God. I appreciate God for opening my eyes and enabling me discover the wonderful gift He had put in me. This is a talent that would have gone unutilised had I not acknowledged You.

The gems in this book and many other things in my life would have remained dormant were it not for my three precious daughters: Corrinne Wairimu Ngurukie, Rachel Nyambura Ngurukie and Yvonne Amy Wanjiru Ngurukie. Their closeness and love has been a great source of encouragement and peace, which has enabled me to concentrate on my writing. They have been such clear mirrors through which I have been able to see through the world, imagine characters and create the story in this and other novels.

Sweethearts, I want you to know that I truly appreciate the advice and support you gave and still give me today; the way you kept on enquiring from me, wanting to know when I would finish writing this book; reading the many drafts I wrote and correcting me where I seemed to have lost my way. You participated in bringing this book to life. Thank you so much. I love you and always will.

Dedication

This book is dedicated to you my precious **daughters**: Corrinne Wairimu Ngurukie, Rachel Nyambura Ngurukie and Yvonne Amy Wanjiru Ngurukie.

CHAPTER

1

◆ ◆ ◆ ◆

The excited Rhodesian people who thronged the local airport of Karuna cheered wildly at the Kenyan peace-keeping troops as they descended from their carriers. This was the eagerly awaited group which was to relieve the first consignment of soldiers who had been dispatched there more than two years ago to monitor the fighting between the Rhodesian Government and the Guerilla Freedom Fighters.

Mrs Pam Kanini Mutisya, staring at the jubilant crowd, descended slowly with her hand luggage. She was not only overwhelmed by the reception accorded to the troops, but was feeling weak and faint from the flight. The strong, relentless heat of the sun that greeted her made her recall with longing the cool, pleasant climate she had left back in Kenya.

So, at last she was in Rhodesia! She wondered excitedly whether her husband, Mutisya, had come to meet her and hoped he had received her last letter to him in which she had confirmed her departure date from Nairobi. Despite her excitement, she also found herself feeling somewhat apprehensive about what her life would be like, both in this strange country so passionately involved in fighting for its freedom, and as the wife of an army officer who was involved in monitoring the fighting. It had been more than two years since she had seen her husband, and sometimes in her day-dreams she grew worried and frightened at the mere thought of what strangers she and her husband might have become. They had known each other for less than a year when they got married. Six days after their hurried marriage, Mutisya had left for Rhodesia with the Kenyan peace-keeping troops, and from then on Kanini had lived on the letters Mutisya had sent her and the memories of the six days she had spent with him as his wife.

Mutisya was a good letter writer and he sent long love letters which were very satisfying to Kanini. In these letters, Mutisya proclaimed his undying love and unshakable loyalty for his wife. He said he missed her very much and longed for the day when he would be re-united with her. '*Kanini muka wakwa* I miss you very much,' he always ended his letters to her.

But for some reason, despite these loving letters from her dear husband, Kanini had her own doubts as to the real reasons why he had not come back home with the others when they ended their two-year service in Rhodesia. He could, she was sure, have been among those who returned home after completing their term of service. And so she had experienced a mixture of both happiness and apprehension when she received a message from the Department of Defence saying that her husband wanted her to go and join him in Rhodesia. She was to be put on the carrier taking the second convoy of troops to Rhodesia.

'Why do you think my husband is not coming home with the others?' she had asked one of Mutisya's fellow officers.

'Madam, I really do not know but I'm sure it is all in the line of duty,' the officer had replied.

'Yes, I suppose it is. You people obey the orders first and then ask questions later!' she put in, smiling. 'In that case, I have no choice but to go where he is then,' she said as she stood up to leave the office.

'You will go in the same carrier that is taking our soldiers to Rhodesia. The details of when they will leave for Rhodesia will be communicated to you, Madam. All the necessary travel documents for you will be processed by this office and will be brought to you as soon as they are ready,' confirmed the officer.

'Thank you very much, Captain er…'

'Captain Ndirangu, Madam,' the officer finished the name for her.

Kanini had a splitting headache. Despite everything she did to control her feelings, she still found herself wondering what had actually brought about this sudden change. Why did Jim want her to go to Rhodesia to join him, rather than him come back home with the others?

She was an only child and although she lived a long distance from her mother, she was solely responsible for looking after her, a duty she fulfilled, despite the distance. Her mother, Mrs Annab Munyao was a sickly woman, although she was not very old. For this reason Kanini was reluctant to go so far away, leaving her alone. Mzee Munyao, Kanini's father and a former senior forest officer, had died five years earlier from a fatal wound caused by a poisoned arrow targeted at him by elephant poachers. The poisoned arrow had taken life out of him instantly, leaving his young widow and only child, Kanini so sad. Since then, Kanini and her mother had become one and really cherished each other.

Kanini knew only too well what it would mean to her mother to see her only daughter leave for a far-away country, especially one at war. Deep down in her heart, Kanini feared that once separated from her mother, she would never see her alive again. This particular thought had discouraged Kanini from accepting her husband's invitation immediately. She felt he understood her dilemma, for part of Mutisya's letter had said,

'My dearest wife, do not forget that I also love your sick mother – for she is my mother too – but I see no reason why you should worry needlessly. I am sure mother is not so selfish as to want to hang on to you all her life. She knows you are a married woman; you are my wife now and, in all fairness, I should have the right to ask you to come over and join me here in Rhodesia. Pam, you are a soldier's wife and you should adapt yourself to the role of a soldier's wife. You must learn to live with sudden changes whenever they occur, because, my dear, changes which radically affect the lives of military personnel and their dependants often take place in this profession. Accepting and adapting to those changes makes all the difference between you, a soldier's wife, and your friends who married civilian husbands.'

Mutisya had deliberately written that paragraph because he knew his wife would find it difficult to leave her mother alone.

'Ah well,' Kanini thought, 'I had expected my life as a soldier's wife would be different from my friends' married to civilian husbands. I had anticipated I would be expected to cope with changes every now and then, but I never expected such an enormous change to come my way so soon. Still, I don't suppose those Rhodesians will fight for long now that there's wind that their independence is just around the corner, so perhaps the peacekeeping troops will soon be pulled out ... '

As for Mutisya, he had loved the country from the minute he set foot on it, although he too had found the unaccustomed strong heat of the sun a bit trying at first. So it had come as a welcomed piece of news that due to his promotion from a major to a lieutenant-colonel he would remain in Rhodesia when the others left for home, and was to become the second in command of the Kenyan troops.

Kanini wondered if she was being mean and selfish by not feeling thrilled that she was soon to join her husband and start a real married life with him, something she had been longing for since their marriage. Of course, it was natural that she should feel upset at leaving her mother, but there were other reasons for her apprehension. She did not want to start her married life with Mutisya in a foreign and war-torn country, especially Rhodesia where it was said that black people were treated like dogs by the white minority who ruled them. She felt that, much as she might try to settle down, she could never be quite happy in this particular country.

'I will not be able to have any children here, much as I want to,' she thought bitterly. The idea of having children awakened, in her, new fears. Jim did not like the idea of having children at all. He was the opposite of Kanini, who longed to bring up her own family. He had already made it plain that he loved his freedom and had no intention of settling down as a father. He loved adventure and was regarded as a confirmed bachelor by his married peers – until fate changed his way of life when he met Pam Kanini.

'What would Jim look like after such a long spell in the scorching heat of Rhodesia?' Kanini wondered. He had looked really handsome in the last photograph he had sent her. It had shown him lounging by a swimming pool in his swimming costume with a glass of wine in his hand. Kanini once more relived the memories that photograph had brought to her, memories of when she first met Mutisya. *'Maybe,'* she thought, *'once I see him the old flame of love and excitement will re-kindle and make me forget my old Mwaitu and all the sadness I feel right now for leaving her behind.'*

'Mrs Mutisya,' a voice called out behind her. She turned and saw Mrs Kate Njoroge coming towards her. Kanini, completely absorbed in her own thoughts, had forgotten all about Mrs Njoroge. However, her face lit up and relaxed into a smile on seeing Kate.

'*Jamaani, Pam nimekutafuta everywhere;*' began Mrs Njoroge, who although had not met Kanini before this day, had got to know her on the plane, and they had found a lot to chat about during their flight.

'*Oh, kweli?*' Kanini found herself wondering that a woman she had just met on the plane should be concerned about her whereabouts.

'*Pole sana,* Kate, if you have been looking for me. I was just wondering how much longer we will have to wait before we can join our soldier husbands,' Kanini said to her, jokingly.

'Ah well, mine is already here!' Kate said excitedly, as she introduced Kanini to her husband, Major Njoroge. Njoroge, like Mutisya, had stayed on when the others left for home.

'*Karibuni* to Rhodesia!' welcomed Major Njoroge, as he shook Kanini's hand.

'*Asante sana,*' replied Kanini.

After seeing to it that their luggage was put in the waiting Land Rover, Major Njoroge invited the ladies to have a drink in a nearby cafe. The day was hot and the idea of a cold drink was welcomed whole-heartedly by both Kate and Pam.

'By the way, I am here to meet both of you,' Major Njoroge said, addressing Kanini in particular. 'The boss had some urgent matters to attend to and he had to make a short journey outside our camp location. However, he was hoping to be back by the time we get there.' Despite her disappointment, Kanini bravely accepted this information as part of the 'sudden changes' she had been warned to expect as an army officer's wife. Meanwhile, Major Njoroge enquired about their flight.

'How did you two find the flight in a carrier?' he asked them.

'It was very lively! We loved every bit of it. Your soldiers were very entertaining and they kept us laughing with their jungle stories all the way,' Kate explained.

'Kenya *gukihaana atia?*' Major Njoroge enquired, in his mother tongue.

'All in Kenya is very well and everybody is following the Nyayo philosophy of "Peace, Love and Unity",' Kanini replied in the same language. Every Kenyan, young or old was well-versed with the president's philosophy and as a requirement, to demonstrate their patriotism, one was required to sing it. Others could go ahead and demonstrate it with the index finger.

'Things here are not as bad either as one would have expected, bearing in mind that there is a war going on between rival freedom fighters and the government troops.'

As Major Njoroge was talking, Kanini found her eyes drawn to his shoulder. How strange that Kate had said her husband was a captain, yet on his shoulder, he wore a major's badge of rank. She was just about to ask Njoroge about his rank when his wife also noticed the change of badge on her husband's shoulder.

'Baba Nyokabi,' Kate called her husband, 'you mean to tell me that you … and you did not even inform me…'

'Yes, Mama Nyokabi,' Major Njoroge replied calmly, 'I got my promotion to Major just over a week ago.'

'That's good. Congratulations!' Kate said, proposing a toast to her husband.

'My congratulations too,' added Pam.

'Thank you. Thank you. As a matter of fact, I think I should also congratulate you too, Mrs Mutisya. Your husband was also promoted to a Lieutenant-Colonel at the same time,' Njoroge told an already excited Pam.

'That's nice. Congratulations, on behalf of your husband, Pam.' Kate proposed another toast, this time for Lieutenant-Colonel Mutisya.

'Oh, thank you! That's good news at least. I'm so happy for Jim!' put in Pam excitedly.

There was silence as each of them disappeared into their own thoughts until Kate suddenly spoke. 'By the way, Baba Nyokabi, tell us what your married quarters are like – I hope they are not tents!'

'You are right Kate,' put in Pam. 'I can cope with anything with a roof, but not a tent!'

'Actually, you have no need to worry! They are not tents, although the mess itself and the NCO's quarters are tents.' Njoroge assured the two ladies. 'Our married quarters,' he went on, 'comprise a one-bedroomed house, a small sitting-room, a kitchen and, of course, a shower and toilet. In fact, they are, really semi-permanent buildings. I am sure you will like them;' he ended, with a big smile.

'How far is your camping site from here?' asked Kate.

'It is quite a distance – about two hundred miles.' Looking at his watch, Major Njoroge suggested it was time they set off if they were to reach the camp before it grew dark.

CHAPTER

2

♦ ♦ ♦ ♦

It was a long journey to the camp, but Njoroge stopped every now and then for the ladies to enjoy beautiful scenery. After several hours of travelling, the three were tired of talking and an easy silence fell upon them. Kanini closed her eyes and tried to sleep. Sleep wouldn't come and she found herself once again reliving all the memories of the first time that she met Mutisya, and of their consequent marriage.

It was on her friend's, Masha Njeri's, wedding day. She was getting married to an airforce officer and Pamela Kanini, who was known to her friends as 'Pam', was her Matron of Honour. Jimmy Mutisya, himself an army officer and a good friend of the groom, was one of the officers who held their swords to form a guard of honour for the bridal party to pass through just after the church nuptials and also on entry at the reception hall. After the reception, there was a dance in the officers' mess.

Mutisya was a marvellous dancer but Kanini could not be out-done; after their first dance together, it was clear they were perfectly matched. Mutisya didn't let her dance with anybody else; Kanini on her part did not mind his monopolising her at all. In fact, she rather liked the idea of the two of them dancing together. Kanini had met many a handsome man before, she felt certain that none was as handsome, as good a dancer, and as interesting to be with as her new acquaintance, Major Mutisya. The way he held her when they danced was so gentle that she almost felt afraid that he would feel her racing heartbeats.

Kanini remembered how, when they had sat down for a rest and a drink, Mutisya had told her about himself. He told her that his name was Jimmy Mutisya and that he was a major in the Kenyan Army, stationed at Nanyuki. She had listened to him attentively and with interest. She remembered too that she had also told him about herself – her full name and that she worked as a secretary with a bank in Nairobi. Kanini recalled Mutisya's reaction when she told him that she felt tired and that she wanted to go home and sleep.

'The evening is just beginning, Pam. What's the hurry?' he asked her.

'I am feeling both sleepy and tired, and I just want to go home and sleep,' she told him again.

'Where do you live, Pam?'

'I live in Buru Buru,' she answered.

'Buru Buru is quite a long way from here. How will you get there?'

'No problem. Njeri's brother will take me.'

'But maybe Njeri's brother wants to go on dancing,' Jim put in.

'He is only dropping me off, and then he can come back and continue dancing ... we've already arranged it that way.'

'In that case, to save the young man the trouble of taking you all the way there and then coming back, why don't I drop you off myself, since I have no intention of dancing after you have gone, Pam?'

'You can't be serious! You've just said that the evening is just beginning – how come you want to go now?' she asked him.

'I hadn't realised it's nearly two in the morning,' he lied, for the late hour had no bearing at all on his change of mind.

On the understanding that Mutisya would take her home, Kanini agreed to dance a few more dances before they left for Buru Buru. In the car, the effects of a long, exciting day made Kanini feel very sleepy, and the soothing country music of Kenny Rogers coming from the car cassette nearly made her doze off. Mutisya was not a fast driver and Kanini felt safe and relaxed.

'Do you live alone in Buru Buru?' his voice cut in.

'No, I shared the house with two of my friends, Njeri and Jelimo, but now that Njeri has married, there's just Jelimo and myself.'

'That sounds rather interesting to me,' Mutisya said.

'Why should it sound interesting to you? Have you never heard of three girls sharing a maisonette?'

'No, it's not that. But girls with very different ethnic backgrounds sharing a house... that's what is interesting. How did it come about, if I may ask?'

'Oh well, that's simple. I am not tribalistic and my friends are not either,' Kanini replied, casually.

'Ah, that's very good,' Mutisya replied, feeling a bit embarrassed by her straightforward answer, which he had not expected.

'You see,' Kanini continued, 'Njeri, Jelimo and I have known each other since our high school days. We went to the same school and then fate brought us together again as working girls here in Nairobi. We decided to share a house as it would be cheaper and safer for each one of us.'

'That's what I call friendship,' Mutisya added with a nod.

For some time both were quiet, and when Mutisya talked again it was all about her beauty and how he had never met a more beautiful girl than her before. 'You are very beautiful Pam ... I am very, very sincere,' Mutisya added. Kanini remained silent.

At last they reached her house. When he stopped the car, Mutisya reached for her hand. 'You've got such lovely soft hands, Pam,' he said in a husky voice that concealed nothing about his admiration for her. Then he suddenly looked straight in her eyes, as if trying to read what she was thinking. 'Pam, I want to see you again, soon. There is something about you which fascinates me. I must see you again. Please don't say no!'

Kanini wanted to tell him that she too wanted to see him again, but she could not get the words out. There was silence, as though each of them was afraid to talk. Kanini was thinking that although she had had boyfriends before, none of them had been so open about her beauty, and she felt thrilled by Mutisya's frankness.

'Well,' she said at last, 'now that you know where I live, you can come around when you next come to Nairobi. You will be sure to find me or Jelimo in, especially in the evenings and on the weekends when I have not gone home.'

'Pam, I don't want to find just somebody in the house, I want to find you!'

'In that case, let me know when you are going to come so that I can wait for you.'

'So many dates to warrant a written appointment, eh?' Mutisya joked.

'I wouldn't say that exactly. I have already told you that I go home to see my mother during some weekends and, of course, on some evenings I may go to watch a movie after work.'

'Don't take me so seriously!' Mutisya was quick to say. 'I was only joking. You see, I'm already beginning to feel jealous in case anybody dates you. Of course, I know you have a boyfriend or boyfriends...'

Kanini did not speak. Then suddenly a loud noise made by a stray dog brought them back to their senses. Even then, when Mutisya spoke, Kanini absent-mindedly stood up from her seat. She had been completely lost in thoughts of what had taken place during the day.

'I'm sorry, Pam, if I sound so concerned but I feel I should tell you exactly what I feel. Today, or was it yesterday – I see it is almost four in the morning – was only our first meeting, but I am already in love with you Pam! Believe it or not, it was love at first sight for me. I really mean it.'

Kanini was still silent. She was only aware of her heart pounding inside her and, afraid of her own feelings, she hurriedly opened the car door. Mutisya was quick to hold her hand and drew her closer to him.

'Pam, please don't go away like that... think about it... I hope I did not offend you or hurt your feelings by being so straight-forward, but that's the way I feel and I cannot hide it. Pam, I just want you to think about it; maybe you can give me an answer later – when I come back. As for now, I will say goodnight and many, many thanks for your charming company.'

'I should be the one to thank you, Major Mutisya. I really...'

'Hold it, Pam! It's "Jim" to you!'

'Well, thank you very much Jim, for everything. It has been

a great pleasure meeting you and spending the day in your company. Goodnight.'

'I will see you to your door, Pam,' he said, as he released her and got out of the car. As soon as he had seen her safely inside the house, he went back to his car and drove off.

Kanini went straight upstairs to her bedroom. She felt completely exhausted and drained by the day's events. She quickly put on her nightdress and got into bed. She tried to sleep, but sleep would not come. She closed her eyes tightly and covered her head, but still sleep seemed to run further and further. Her body was tired but her mind was wide awake and restless. She found herself thinking about Mutisya and all that he had told her. '*Hmmmm ... Major Mutisya ... no, no, Jim – "It's 'Jim' to you,"*' she played the entire scene in her mind. '*And Jim is in love with me! My goodness, how fate brings two people together nobody can explain!*' She then visualised herself marrying Mutisya, going through the guard of honour just like her friend, Njeri ... '*Oh God ... I think I am going crazy! I wish I could lay my hands on some sleeping pills ... I swear I would take ten of them if it would only make me go into a deep sleep!*'

At this point, Kanini was not quite sure whether she was feeling cold or if she was sick. She felt like shivering, yet she thought she was warm enough. It was a cold night, so she decided to get up and fetch the heater to warm the room. Slowly she went downstairs to the sitting-room and took the heater. She plugged it in, switched on the bedside light and lay on her bed, wide awake. She heard the cock crow and cursed under her breath.

'*What on earth is wrong with me? What's happened to my sleep?*

Goodness me, it will soon be day and I'll still be awake!' The whole room was now warm but Kanini could not go to sleep.

Her mind wandered uncontrollably; for no apparent reason, she imagined Mutisya being killed in one of the horrific Shifta wars – she had visions of his body being blown into tiny pieces by the landmines planted by the Shiftas and she almost screamed out loud. Her body was cold and trembling with fear as she tried to force the ugly thought out of her mind. Try as she did, she could not avoid thinking about him. She imagined him dancing a slow waltz with her, his eyes fixed on hers, his narrow eyes concealing nothing of the admiration he felt for her. No other man, she thought, had made her feel the way Mutisya made her feel. But despite all those wild thoughts and the wishful thinking, Kanini was certain of one thing – Jim would never come back, she would never see him again. Their meeting had just been by chance, and Jim would not be back.

'*I'm sure he's got several girlfriends, and it is stupid of me to think that I will be his only girlfriend – if I am to be one at all!*' she thought sarcastically, but at the same time she felt faint and very sad at the thought of perhaps never seeing him again. It was nearly morning when Kanini at last dismissed all the foolish thoughts and wishful thinking and fell asleep.

Mutisya did actually go back to see her. That very Sunday afternoon, before he left for Nanyuki, he decided to go and see Pam and take her out for a drink. Kanini had just woken up when Jim showed up, and after her restless night she did not feel like going anywhere. Jim used all his charms to persuade her to go out with him for a drink in the officers' mess.

Being on a Sunday, there were not very many people in the mess and after a few sodas, Jim suggested that they go to eat at Dagoretti Corner. He felt hungry and knew that Kanini was hungry too. At Dagoretti, Jim recognised a few officers but turned down their invitation to join them. He wanted to be with Pam. While they both sat in his car and ate goat meat which Jim had ordered, Pam heard a lot more about Mutisya. He was the first son of Pastor Paul Kyalo and Mrs Ruth Wanza Kyalo of Kangundo. Kanini knew and remembered Mrs Ruth Kyalo as the kind old lady who had been very consoling and helpful to her mother when her father died. Mrs Kyalo had said prayers almost every night in Kanini's house before and even after the burial. She was, therefore, very surprised to learn that this same Mrs Kyalo was Mutisya's mother. She would never have guessed that the kind old lady was Jim's mother! Kanini had heard a lot about the pastor's family before from her mother, but she had not been very interested – after all, they did not live near enough to be neighbours. The parents only knew one another through their church activities.

Kanini heard that Pastor Kyalo had wanted his son to become a doctor, but Mutisya, a sixth-former then, had cultivated his own interests in the field of defence. He wanted to be an army officer. His uncle, Kimeu, now a retired warrant officer, had managed to convince Mutisya that a career in the Armed Forces was the best. He told Mustisya many thrilling stories about how he'd fought in Burma during the World War II, and about the most recent war waged by Shifta guerillas in the then North Eastern Province of Kenya. It was both fun and dangerous being involved in such action, his uncle had told him with a lot of excitement.

Apart from war stories, Kimeu had also told Mutisya many funny stories, including the legendary one about why the Akamba outnumbered other tribes in the Armed Forces.

'To begin with,' Mzee Kimeu had told his nephew, 'in the early days when Africans were joining what was then the King's African Rifles, the first to join were the Akamba, and then later on other tribes like the Gikuyu and the Luo started joining. These other tribes never got very far and very few managed to finish the strenuous training. This failure of other tribes, to be frank, was not because they were physically weak or inferior. The actual reason was they could not understand the training officers' language of instruction. Those involved in training the recruits used funny tricks when conducting drills in the field. During the drill, the Mkamba instructor would begin like this: "By the left, qui... ick march! Left! Right! Left! Right! Left... " Then when everybody was in step, he would suddenly change and say: *'Kwa aka! Kwa aume! Kwa aka! Kwa aume!'* Now this sudden change to Kikamba would confuse everybody except the Akamba recruits, who would understand and march on uninterrupted whilst everybody else made a mess of the drill by falling out of step. When it came to command an 'about-turn' and then march on, the drill sergeant major would shout to the recruits, *'Itina!'* meaning 'about-turn'. He would then carry on. *'Kwa aka! Kwa aume! Kwa aka! Kwa aume!'* The recruits who understood the language would make an about-turn and continue marching, while the others who did not understand the instructions would continue marching straight on!'

Such stories thrilled Mutisya very much and he laughed every time he remembered this particular story. And by the time Mutisya had finished telling this story to Kanini, she had laughed so much that she nearly choked on her food. She liked the lively and animated way he told the story, '*Mutisya has a good sense of humour,*' she thought.

'I really enjoy your stories!' she said, still laughing and begged him to tell her another of his jokes.

'If you want me to tell you more,' Mutisya said, 'then promise me, on your honour, that you will not break any of your ribs by laughing!'

'I promise, on my honour, that I will not break any of my ribs... ' Kanini said, imitating the solemn promise of girl guides.

'You must have been a girl guide, Pam,' he told her.

'And you must have been a boy scout,' she told him.

'Well, never mind whether I was or wasn't,' he told her. 'All I wanted was your solemn promise, and I got it! Now Pam, tell me, how often do you read the "Today in Parliament" column in the papers?'

'Why do you ask that, Jim?' Kanini asked in astonishment.

'Well, no reason in particular, but just answer my question.'

'To be honest,' she told him, 'I never read that page at all because I think it is all politics and I am not at all interested in politics. Don't they say that politics is a dirty game, Jim?'

'Yes, politics can be a dirty game but only if the politicians themselves are dirty. They are the ones who defile it. However, this column is not all politics. There is a lot of interesting information. Pam, on this particular page one can learn a lot from our Honourable Members of Parliament; sometimes they lose their tempers with each other and other times they make jokes. Do you know what "Monday Blues" are Pam?'

'Yes, I think ... a hangover from the weekend drinking, and all the misery that goes with it.'

'Yeah, that's right. Well, I was nursing one of them – a real king-sized hangover – when a friend of mine opened my office door and came in laughing like a fool (at least that's what I thought of him then, a fool).'

'What's so funny? That newspaper you are holding?' I asked him. 'Yes,' he answered. I found it hard to believe that a full captain could find a newspaper quite so funny. 'Hey, Alakani,' I warned him, 'I am in no laughing mood...' but despite that, the guy continued laughing, opened his newspaper and started reading.

'This,' he began, 'is the Honourable Member for Matopeni East Constituency asking the Honourable Minister for Defence to explain how his ministry recruits soldiers in the armed forces. Listen to this, the Honourable Member for Matopeni East Constituency during question time, 'Mr Speaker, Sir, would the Honourable Minister tell this House where recruits are drawn from, because for quite some time now there have been no such recruitments in my Constituency?' The Honourable Minister stood up and directly addressed the Honourable Member for Matopeni East, *'Kwa Nyukwa*, everywhere in our republic'. And then this usually sober captain burst into uncontrollable fits of laughter again!' Jim finished his story triumphantly.

Kanini knew the Gikuyu language very well and knew the words the Honourable Minister had used when literally translated meant 'from your mothers', and that this was a bad joke and was intended to insult the Matopeni East Member of Parliament. But for Pam, the joke was a very funny one indeed, especially as Jim had told it using the exaggerated tone of a politician.

'Jim,' Kanini managed to say after she had stopped laughing, 'tell me, is "Alakani" a rank in the army?'

Knowing what it meant, Jim could not help but laugh. 'There you are, my dear, making another joke.'

'Why are you laughing? What's the joke?' Pam asked him innocently.

'"Alakani", my dear, is just a nickname a group of us gave ourselves to symbolise that we were in one intake, we graduated together, and what's more – we were very good friends and still are... that's all there is to it, Pam.'

Both were silent for a moment and then, looking at his watch, Jim decided it was high time he started his journey back to Nanyuki.

'*Sasa* Pam, I have to be on my way back to the barracks,' he told her. 'However, the next time I come down to see you, I will tell you more of my stories!'

'But Jim, tell me a few more before you go,' she begged him. 'At least one more... '

After telling Pam the last joke, Jim drove her to her Buru Buru house and left for Nanyuki. He promised to ring soon and tell her when he would be back in Nairobi again.

Two weeks passed by and Kanini heard nothing from Mutisya.

'*These men are all the same, no matter how different they try to be! They all make empty promises, and want to be taken as different from others!*' Kanini lay down on her bed one Saturday morning, thinking. '*Well,*' she thought, '*he fooled me and made me believe that he was different from others – and he's an army officer who is supposed to be well-disciplined and trustworthy. I certainly fell for his tricks, completely forgetting what a friend of mine told me once that army men were labelled the "Three W's", meaning "War, Wine and Women!" Gosh, I will never trust anyone of them, never again! And as for Njeri... poor Njeri, too late, she has already tied a knot with one of them ... what a disaster!*' Pam's thoughts were interrupted by a knock on the door.

Kanini was so absorbed in her day-dreaming that the soft knock on the door literally made her jump from her bed. She grabbed her dressing-gown and ran downstairs to open the door without stopping to think. She had no idea how long she had been lying on that bed, and thought at first that her friend, Jelimo, had locked herself outside. Then suddenly Pam remembered that Jelimo was supposed to be at her brother's wedding – in fact Pam was to attend it later during the day to help serve the guests. Then just before she opened the door, she looked at her watch. It was ten in the morning. '*Ah,*' she comforted herself, '*I still have plenty of time!*' The reception was not until two-thirty in the afternoon.

'Hi! Hello, Pam! And how are you?' Jim greeted her as she opened the door. 'Er... well, I am... I'm fine. Please, come in,' she invited him.

'I'm sorry, Pam, to have called on you like this without any notification. I hope I haven't disrupted your sleep,' said Jim apologetically, noticing her dressing-gown.

'Well, I can't really say you disrupted my sleep because I should have been awake long ago – in fact, your waking me up is a good thing! Please do come right in,' she invited him again.

'I'm relieved ... ' said Jim with a sigh as he went in.

'Do sit down and make yourself comfortable, and if you will excuse me, I will be back in a moment. Help yourself to the music, and you might like to look at this.' She handed him a big photo album and then she went upstairs.

Kanini felt embarrassed that Mutisya, of all the people, should find her dressed in a housecoat – and an unwashed face! She went straight to the bathroom and took a warm bath. Then she dressed in clean jeans and a white shirt. Soon she joined Mutisya in the sitting room.

'You look beautiful in those jeans, Pam,' he complimented her as soon as she appeared. 'Look, I feel awfully sorry to bother you ...' he was beginning to say, but Pam interrupted him.

'No, no, there is nothing to be sorry for, Jim. In fact, I should be grateful to you that you came when you did. I meant to wake up earlier, but... '

'Then you have a date?' asked Mutisya.

'Yes, as a matter of fact I have a date – and a very important one at that.' 'Oh, then I should be on my way, or your date will...'

'No, you don't have to go or worry about my date because I am not going out until after midday,' Kanini told him.

'But then he will...'

'He! Who is he?' Kanini asked him in astonishment.

'Well, your date of course. Who else?' Mutisya replied rather sharply.

'Whatever you are thinking, you are very wrong, Jim. Tell me, why is it that you men think that a girl can only have a date with a man? I mean it's so absurd!'

'Jealousy. That's what it is. A man has to be jealous.'

'My goodness! Jealous of what?'

'Many things, I suppose. Anyway, Pam, tell me who your date is today.'

Pam, not wanting to argue about it further, explained to Jim all about her commitments that day.

'You remember my friend Jelimo, the girl I share this house with? Her brother is getting married today and I'm going to help with serving the guests after the ceremony which, as I have already told you, will be after midday.'

'Of course, I remember that name very well. Where is the reception?' he asked.

'It is in Taifa Hall,' she told him. 'By the way, can I offer you something to eat? I have not yet had my breakfast, so if you don't mind I will go and get some tea for both of us from the kitchen.'

Kanini went to the kitchen to prepare some tea and left Mutisya looking through the photo album. As she made the tea, Pam thought, '*Men! Ah, men are funny creatures! You only need to mention the word "date" and they turn green with jealousy. It doesn't even occur to them that a girl might have a date with another girl to go to a movie or something like that. They think dates are made with men, and men alone. Funny creatures they are, with such little minds'*. Her thoughts were interrupted by Mutisya's voice behind her.

'Pam, can I give you a helping hand?'

'Oh, no. Thank you. I will manage. In fact, I don't have much to do; it seems Jelimo had taken care of my breakfast before she left. There is some tea in the flask and some drop scones in the oven,' she said, as he picked up the tray on which she had put the flask and the plate with the drop scones. On reaching the sitting room, Kanini took out two cups from the cabinet and served herself and Mutisya with tea.

'Now,' Mutisya began, 'remember I told you men can be jealous of many things?'

'Yes, you told me that, but I cannot understand why,' Pam replied.

'Well, I will tell you why I'm particularly jealous about any other man dating you.' He drew closer to Pam. 'Pam, I'm in love with you. I have loved you ever since I saw you at that wedding. You have completely conquered my heart. Pam, there is something about you which I cannot resist. You are so different from anyone else I've met.'

Unlike many other girls of her age who would have melted immediately at Mutisya's loving words, Pam remained silent, trying to digest all that Mutisya had told her.

'Don't you believe me, Pam?' he asked her at last.

'Well, I'm not quite sure I do, because...' He cut her short.

'Pam, you'd better believe me! I mean every word I'm telling you. Listen Pam, I know what you are thinking...'

'What am I thinking?' she asked him.

'Come on, Pam, look at me. Listen, I know you are thinking that I am just another of those men full of sweet talk for young girls like you, when in fact they don't mean a thing that they say. Well, I am not that kind of a person and if you only knew me, Pam, you would not think of me in such a way.'

There was silence as Kanini poured herself another cup of tea and sat up to drink it.

'At least say something, Pam,' he urged her.

Still Kanini kept silent. But her mind was racing as she frantically tried to find the words to answer Mutisya.

'I'm sorry if I've said too much, Pam, but that's the way I feel. Please, if I've offended you by coming without any notice, I'm sorry. '

'Jim, I've already said there's no reason to be sorry,' Kanini spoke at last. 'My being quiet does not in any way mean that I am annoyed with your coming here. You see, it's just that I don't know whether to believe you or not – especially you army officers...'

'Why, Pam? Why not us army officers? Are you suggesting that army men are not capable of loving a woman, or do you mean to say they are not worthy of being loved?' Mutisya asked her in astonishment.

'Well, not exactly... it's just that they are... ' she hesitated.

'They are what, Pam? Come on, tell me!' he demanded.

'It's just that they are reputed to be lovers of women, wine and war. They are never honest – at least, that's what I have heard.'

'Oh, Pam, Pam! Come off it! You mean to tell me that that bad joke about the three W's has such an effect on a sensible girl like you? Oh, Pam... how can I explain it? Look here, Pam, civilian people who really don't know what it means to be in the armed forces, have the nerve to say that army officers only think of war, and if there is no war, they think of wine and women. You have no idea how untrue it is... these fellows just want to discredit the whole armed forces with their rotten mentality. That, I can tell you, Pam, is a very bad joke and it gives a totally wrong impression of an army officer. I hope you are not one of those people who think of us that way.' He paused and there was silence. Then he continued, 'It's funny to think that the same civilians will wonder why we say we are busy, or feel tired because of too much work. "Busy doing what?" they ask. "You people are so idle! All you do is drills, and cleaning your boots and guns, that's all! And then you get free beer, free food, free everything! You guys are so lucky!" That's what most civilian men say about us,' Jim tried to explain to Pam.

There was still silence as Pam tried to put another record on the player. Then Mutisya continued. 'You know, one day I was talking to a civilian acquaintance of mine – not someone one would call a friend – and I told him how tired I felt that particular evening because I had been very busy the whole day, in the office. And you know what? The man looked me straight in the eyes and said, "You must be joking! You've been busy doing what? You guys are so idle! There is no war, despite the rumours of war. I just wish you could have as many files in your in-tray as I do – that is if you even know what a file is!" Pam, I could hardly believe my ears when I heard him say that. The whole thing was such an insult to me and to the entire armed forces. When I asked him exactly what he meant by it, he replied, I mean just that. You guys just have to report to the field and go through the drills for two hours or so in the morning, and that's it! After that you go to clean your guns and boots, day in, day out, until the end of the month and then you get your fat pay packet!" the stupid man continued, "And as if that was not enough, you get free drinks, free food and even free wives!" Well, I was just lost for words!' Jim finished.

Here, Pam could not help it, she just burst out laughing. 'I may not know much about you armed forces men, but I certainly don't think that is what the government has employed you to do. And what's more, I know for a fact that my friend Masha Njeri's husband paid some dowry to her parents.'

'Thank goodness!' Jim said. 'At least you are not so naive, Pam. How grown people calling themselves men can be so stupid and naive is beyond me. It just shows how ignorant some people are. They don't realise we have administrative offices to man, just like any other government ministry in this country.'

The conversation took a lighter turn and they chatted for half an hour or so, whilst in the background Skeeter Davis' songs played quietly, complaining of how she had been let down by love so many times. Kanini, looking at her watch, began clearing the table, then she excused herself to go and get ready so she would not be late for the reception.

Kanini was soon back in the sitting room, dressed in a beautiful cream chiffon outfit which perfectly complemented her fair complexion. She looked beautiful.

'Wow! And all that just to serve guests!' exclaimed Mutisya. 'You really look gorgeous. I hope the groom does not change his mind and pick you out to be his bride!' he joked.

'Don't be silly, Jim.'

'If I were him, I think I would; you look so beautiful and irresistible, Pam. But then, thank goodness, by the time the groom sees you he will have already vowed to take someone else to be his wedded wife. Anyway, can I have the privilege of dropping you at the reception?' he asked.

'Yes, I wouldn't mind a lift there, if you are free, Jim.'

'What do you mean? Of course I'm free! And by the way, what time do you think the reception will end?'

'Why do you want to know?' she asked him, knowing the answer full well.

'Because I want to come and pick you up Pam, that's why.' 'Thanks Jim, but I can't really say what time it will end. You know how it is with wedding receptions, never keeping to time —except the ones that are organised by you people!' she joked.

'In that case, let's say I'll come at around five-thirty, just to check.'

'Well yes, if you'd like to, come any time between five-thirty and six. Thank you very much, Jim; it's a very kind offer.'

CHAPTER

3

◆ ◆ ◆ ◆

Mutisya dropped Kanini at the Taifa Hall with the promise to check on her later in the evening. Everything looked very impressive. The hall itself was beautifully decorated, both outside and inside, ready to receive the bridal party and guests. Like most weddings, the bridal party did not keep to time, and arrived at the hall just after three o'clock – nearly two hours late. Most people were already very hungry, as no food or drinks could be served before the arrival of the bridal party. So immediately after the arrival of the bridal party, Pam and her group of servers were as busy as bees serving food and drinks. Soon everybody had eaten and the dirty dishes removed from the tables. Next, there was the cake-cutting ceremony, which was one of its own. The bridegroom gave his bride traditional food, food from a man to his wife. This was well-grilled lamb ribs. Then the bride gave her husband a different kind of traditional food - a well mashed mixture of various vegetables and *njahi* as befitted a good husband. This traditional food was topped with sour porridge, served in a traditional calabash.

After the 'cake-cutting' ceremony, it was time to present the newly-weds with gifts from relatives and friends, followed by a vote of thanks from the master of ceremonies.

Finally the reception ended. According to Pam's watch, it was fifteen minutes to six o'clock when she hurried out to check whether Jim had arrived. Just as she stepped outside, she spotted Mutisya's car parked almost opposite the main entrance to the hall.

Jim was deep in a conversation with another man, who was leaning against the car. From the way both men were talking, Kanini could tell that they were not just acquaintances, but very good friends.

'Am I early or late?' Jim asked Pam as she approached them.

'You are not either; you are just on time! The reception has just ended,' she replied.

'Sam... meet Pam. Pam; this is Sam, a very good, old friend of mine,' Jim introduced them.

'It's a pleasure to meet you, Pam,' Sam said extending his hand to greet Kanini.

'You too, Sam,' she replied as she shook his hand.

'Pam,' Sam continued, 'I was just asking my friend here when we can expect him to invite us to an occasion like this. He is not getting any younger – I don't know what he's waiting for. Perhaps you tell me, Pam?'

A deathly hush followed and Pam felt her face grow hot with embarrassment. She looked at Jim for help but it seemed he did not intend to let the chance pass.

'Yes, Pam, can you help me answer Sam's question?'

This unexpected suggestion from Jim not only made Pam feel even more embarrassed, but made her angry too. '*We hardly know each other,*' she thought, '*and now he's put me in a very awkward position, especially in front of a stranger.*'

'How can I help you answer Sam's question, Jim?' she asked him quietly, struggling to hide her embarrassment.

'I mean, tell him when you want us to... you know... when do you think you and I can invite him and many others to a ceremony like this?' Jim said, as he took Pam's hand in his and looked her straight in the eyes.

Pam did not know what to say or do. She could not have spoken even if she'd known what to say. She just kept quiet and looked down. It was Mutisya who spoke at last.

'Ah well, very soon we will let you know Sam.'

'I only hope you mean business this time, Jim. You have been a bachelor for too long. You know,' Sam sounded very serious now, 'apart from you and I think Peter, who has lived in the States for all these years, all our other classmates are married with a family of two or three children,' Sam said.

'Oh really! All the same, thanks Sam. I really appreciate your concern about my personal welfare. Let's hope that things will work out fine,' Jim told Sam.

'*Hapo Kibao,* Jim! I wish you good luck, Pam,' Sam called her, 'take care of my good friend, Jim. He's not such a bad boy!'

'I will try Sam,' she answered shyly.

When all was said and done, Kanini had to admit that she was in love with Mutisya. She had not known before what love can do to a person. She was now beginning to see that things can be very different when one was in love; people in love live in a world of their own, and Kanini was no exception.

Their love affair was in its fifth month when things took a different turn. All of a sudden and without much notice, Mutisya was informed that he was one of the officers who had been chosen to go to what was then Rhodesia with the Peace-Keeping Force. The Rhodesians were still waging a guerilla war against each political party, and until there was peace as witnessed by neutral forces, there would be a delay in granting independence to that country. At a meeting, it was agreed that some states, including Kenya, should send their armed forces as observers of the situation. So it was that Major Mutisya and many other officers and servicemen were to go to Rhodesia. They were to leave in a month's time.

When Mutisya broke the news of his departure to Kanini, she wept openly. She thought of the war-torn country which she had so often read about in the newspapers, and imagined him killed... blown into small fragments by a landmine... She found the thought unbearable.

She loved him, he was the man she would always love and wanted to marry; she could not live without him. What was she going to do? Day and night, Kanini thought of nothing else, nobody else, not even her sickly mother. Her love for Jim had changed her so much. The quiet Kanini, who thought her love for her mother could never be equalled, was now experiencing a different kind of love that was greater and different from what she felt for her mother.

Mutisya too, had his own thoughts. His were unpleasant, and were mainly dominated by the worry that he might die in the war-torn country. This thought alone made him decide that he must get married before he left for Rhodesia, so that even if he was killed at least he would leave a wife behind him, and who knows, there might even be a child... a son, perhaps, who would carry on his name.

All the soldiers and officers drawn from various units to go to Rhodesia were given a month's leave so that they could sort out their immediate family affairs, since it was not-officially known how long they would be outside the country. Mutisya did not waste any time, and immediately went to see Kanini to discuss the possibility of a quick marriage.

'*Thank goodness*,' Mutisya thought, '*Kanini is not a total stranger to my family and I'm no stranger to her mother!*' They had decided to visit their respective families soon after their initial meeting, and therefore were known to be friends. Their old folks suspected it was more than just friendship since it was the first time either had brought a friend of the opposite sex home. So the news that they wished to get married was sure to be welcomed by both families, especially Mutisya's who had of late pestered him to find himself a girl and get married. Kanini had, no doubt, impressed his family on their first visit to his home. She was a very pleasant and likeable girl, and Mutisya's mother in particular had received her with open hands, for Mutisya's mother knew Kanini's family very well. Similarly, and by sheer coincidence, when they visited Kanini's mother, the old lady had taken a liking to Mutisya and knew him as their local preacher's son. She too had sensed that he must be her daughter's special friend.

'I don't know how you feel about the whole thing Pam, but I suggest that when we go home and talk to our folks and try to arrange an immediate marriage, we do not mention the short time we have known each other. To me, the length of time we have known each other does not matter – it does not make any difference. We could have met many years ago or yesterday. Pam, what matters is the love we have for each other. I love you, Pam, and I hope you feel that way for me.'

All the time Mutisya talked, Kanini was tongue-tied. Her mind was a whirlwind of confusion, not knowing which direction to blow. She was trying to think through the whole idea, but could not come anywhere near reaching a conclusion. She did not know what to say at all, much as she wanted to say something to Mutisya.

'Look, Pam,' Jim broke the silence, 'I know it is all too hasty for you but we, you and I, have to make a decision before we go home. I mean we must have something to tell our folks. Surely if you really love me, Pam, then... '

'I love you, Jim, and you know it... but... '

'But what, Pam? If you love me as much as I love you, then it should not be very difficult for you to decide.'

'Jim... I don't know... I really don't know. I mean…'

'Listen, Pam. As I told you before, I am leaving in a month's time and that is about all the time we have to come to a decision. You and I have to decide, and the sooner we do it the better! I, already have made up my mind that I want to marry you, Pam.'

'Jim, do you know how long you will be expected to stay in Rhodesia?'

'No. I don't know that and nobody else knows either. It will depend on when the fighting stops, and that is so unpredictable, especially because it's a guerilla war against a powerful party. It might take one month, two, one year, two years - we really don't know.'

'Oh dear!' she sighed. 'That makes things even more difficult.'

'Yes, I am afraid so, Pam.'

There was silence again as Kanini struggled to gather her thoughts together to find an answer to Mutisya's suggestion. 'Well,' she finally said, 'if you are really serious, Jim, then I have no objection to your plans. But I really don't know how I will approach my mother.'

'Pam,' he spoke gently, 'you know I am serious and I mean every word that I have said. As for your mother, well, we will think of the right way to approach her. I know it will be a shock to her but we will find a solution. I'm sure once you and I have agreed on everything; our parents will not be a problem.'

It was quite late when at last the two parted ways after lengthy discussions about their marriage. Fortunately, it was on a Friday night and Kanini did not have to work the next day. It was already nine in the morning when Kanini woke up. She had to prepare very fast and go to meet Mutisya. As they had agreed the previous night, they left for Kangundo. They had arranged that their first stop should be at Kanini's home. Kanini would be left there to break the news to her mother, while Mutisya proceeded to his home to tell them not only that he was going to Rhodesia, but also about the consequent arrangements for his immediate marriage to Kanini.

As the couple had anticipated, the news of Mutisya's immediate marriage was whole-heartedly welcomed by both his father and mother, but the reaction of Kanini's mother to the marriage couldn't have been more different. It was bad news to the old lady, for she had never spared a moment to think that her only daughter and child would one day grow and get married. The news came to her as a great shock.

'My daughter,' she said to Kanini, close to tears, 'you are my only child. How can you think of marriage at your age? To marry and go away from me, your mother, with nobody to stay with and take care of me. Kanini, why do you want to marry and leave me alone... is there anything that I have refused to give you or denied you that you think only a man can give you?'

Despite her failing health, Mrs Munyao was a wealthy woman. Her late husband had left a substantial sum of money for her, and she lived a very comfortable kind of life. As far as the villagers were concerned, being the owner of a very nice permanent stone house on a very big farm was very luxurious. This was a preserve of a few. She had also inherited shares in several businesses of which her late husband was a director.

'*Mwaitu*,' Kanini addressed her mother in her own language, 'I do not want to marry Mutisya because I am lacking anything. I just want to make a home, a home for myself. You yourself like Mutisya – you told me so. *Mwaitu*, please try to understand, I…'

'But you are only a child, Kanini,' her mother lamented.

'*Mwaitu*, you may think that I am only a child; every mother always thinks that way, that their daughters are always babies who are never grown up enough to make their own homes. But *Mwaitu*, I am twenty-five years old and that is old enough,' Kanini told her mother, convincingly.

'You love this man, Kanini, don't you?' asked her mother.

'Yes, *Mwaitu*. I love him very much, but you must understand that the way I love him is not the way I love you. You are my mother and my getting married to Mutisya will not change my love for you.'

'I know my dear daughter. You see, it is very difficult for a mother, especially one like myself with only one child, to think that their only child is going away. I could not control myself. Of course I know Mutisya is a fine man, born and brought up in a Christian family, but you see it has come much too soon…I mean, I could not think of him wanting to marry you so soon…'

'*Mwaitu*, Mutisya is not taking me away from you. We are only getting married. I am not going to Rhodesia with him – he is leaving me right here. You need not be afraid of that.'

'Oh!' Mrs Munyao expressed some satisfaction. 'Then is he not taking you with him to Rhodesia?'

'No, *Mwaitu*, he is not,' Kanini answered, knowing she had finally won her mother over.

'Ahaaaa,' sighed Mrs Munyao again, 'that makes a big difference! Now tell me, Kanini, has Mutisya told his parents about this yet?'

'That is what he has gone to tell them today. We agreed that I would break the news to you myself, while he goes to talk to his parents.'

'In that case, my child, let's wait and hear what his parents have to say. I will give you my answer then.'

The following day when Mutisya arrived at Kanini's home to pick her up, he was to hear the news that although her mother had been shocked and upset to hear the news of the intended marriage of her only child and daughter, the old lady was not totally opposed to the idea, and she would give her answer after hearing the reaction of Mutisya's parents.

'My son,' Mrs Munyao had called Mutisya, 'I have known your parents for a long time as very good Christians. I have no doubt that if you have taken after any of them you are a good child.' There was silence as the old lady seemed to be deep in thoughts for a moment, and then she spoke again. 'I have already told Kanini that before Christianity spread to us, our clan did not inter-marry with your clan. There was a bad curse and it was believed that if such a marriage took place, it resulted in the couple not bearing any children at all. That is now all gone and forgotten, thanks to the first Christians who brought us the good news. We no longer believe in those things, though some still do believe in them even today, I mean those who are still in the dark.' There was another quiet moment and then Mrs Munyao spoke again. 'If I can remember right, Kanini told me that you are on a three-week leave during which you have to arrange for your marriage?'

'Yes, mother, I have only three weeks,' Mutisya replied shyly.

'Well, as you know our custom, there is not much that I can discuss with you but I suggest that your parents, myself and Kanini's uncles meet to talk about it all, this is not something that I can handle alone. It will only be then that we can discuss this matter further,' Kanini's mother told Mutisya.

'Yes, mother,' Mutisya replied, with relief.

As was Mrs Munyao's habit when her daughter came to visit her, she had packed some green vegetables from the farm, some fruits, an enormous bottle of fresh cow's milk and some sieved honey for her daughter to take back with her. Kanini's mother strongly believed that honey was the best drink for anybody to take when they felt thirsty, especially the young and growing children. She always urged her daughter to drink it. For Mutisya, she gave him a live hen – a sign of good luck.

'Mwanzia!' Mrs Munyao called her shamba boy. 'Mwanzia, come here! Put these things in the car.'

CHAPTER

4

◆ ◆ ◆ ◆

It was four o'clock in the afternoon when Mutisya and Kanini finally left for Nairobi, and on the journey each of them told the other their family's reactions on hearing the news of their intended marriage.

'As I expected,' Mutisya began, 'my parents were thrilled when I told them I wanted to get married. My mother, just like any other mother who has taken a liking to a particular girl and wishes her son would marry the girl and bring her home to be her daughter-in-law, was quick to say, "I hope it is to that Munyao's daughter!" Imagine that, Pam! She loves you that much. You should have seen the happiness in her eyes when I told her that it was none other but you! And by the way, Pam, my old man told me that he and your late father were very good friends. He told me how your father was a good Christian and never drank alcohol. Typical of those church elders – the first things they want to know about someone is whether they drink alcohol, smoke cigarettes and if they circumcise their daughters. Your family, my father told me, has a good reputation. I was really impressed and I told myself, "Congratulations to you, Jim Mutisya! You couldn't have made a better choice!"'

All the while that Jim talked, Pam was quiet. She too was thinking how lucky she was to find Mutisya, a man from a Christian family to marry her.

'What would you expect the church elders to do? I mean, they do not drink themselves, so they have to know who drinks and who does not,' Kanini put in.

'Oh, but some do drink, my dear Kanini,' Mutisya told her. 'Then they are not true Christians! They must be bogus ones!' she said.

'No, no, my dear Pam, they are genuine ones. Don't you know that some churches allow their members to drink?'

'Really?' asked Kanini in astonishment.

'Yes, they do. Some allow their priests to drink too.'

'Well! I had no idea that drinking was allowed - in any Christian Church, for that matter... I mean, to allow them to drink openly.'

For a moment there was silence, save for the car engine and the soft music coming from the car cassette – Skeeter Davis still complaining about her unfortunate love affairs. Then Mutisya spoke.

'My parents,' he began, 'decided that they would arrange a day this week to go and see your mother. In fact, I am going back there tomorrow so that we can fix the day and time together. What I suggest is that you take your leave, because although your presence will not be needed during the dowry negotiations, you will need to be free to make other preparations for the wedding. You see, my dear, I am that confident that your people will bless us and agree to our marriage just as my own people have done, and not cause unnecessary delays.'

Kanini agreed with him and, prompted by Mutisya, went on to tell him more, how her mother had reacted to the news she told her.

'Well,' Kanini began, 'she was not as thrilled with the news as your parents, because, in the first place, my marriage to you or anybody else would mean my going away from our homestead for good. To tell you the truth, Jim, I expected this kind of reaction from her anyway. Wouldn't any mother react in the same way? You know how they feel, the mothers. They always feel that their daughters are not big enough to be on their own; they always think of them as their "little girl". Mothers have this strong feeling that they are losing their daughters for ever. Anyway, I did try to explain to her that my marriage to you would not mean my not taking care of her anymore, but in fact it would mean the two of us looking after her. And, because I knew her greatest fear was that I might be going with you to Rhodesia, I told her that I was not going with you but would remain right here. She also wanted to know how safe you would be out there, and I explained that you and all the others from our country were not going to be actively involved in the fighting but you were going as observers and would be far from the war zones. That put her mind at rest and softened her a little. Anyway, the conclusion is as you heard her say. A meeting with your folks, herself and my immediate uncles.'

'That's not at all a bad conclusion. At least there is plenty of room for hope,' Mutisya said happily.

Mutisya drove slowly and carefully while listening to what Pam said. It was very late in the evening when they got to Buru Buru, both feeling so tired but very happy indeed. The following day, which was on a Monday, Mutisya drove back to Kangundo where his parents, uncles and aunts were waiting for him to discuss his marriage and to arrange a day when they could go to Kanini's home. The day was agreed upon and a message was sent to Mrs Munyao through Mutisya to Kanini. As is the custom, when a girl whose father is dead is getting married, her late father's brothers act as the girl's father. A few close clansmen are also called to meet with the suitor's parents and clansmen to discuss the dowry. Like in most African communities, the dowry is usually set by the girl's family.

Without wasting time, Mutisya drove Kanini to her home two days after to inform her mother of the decision. Kanini had already applied for her annual leave which was granted immediately. On receiving the news of the visit by Mutisya's people, Kanini's mother knew that the two young people were serious. They wanted to get married. She went to inform her late husband's brother, Mzee Kitema, of the matter. After a lengthy discussion, which was mainly about Mutisya's background, Mzee Kitema agreed to inform their close clansmen and to invite them to his late brother's homestead on the appointed day to meet with Mutisya's people. They were coming to *kwitya munuu* – to ask for the girl's hand in marriage.

Although both sides were Christians, the traditional ritual of cooking of the traditional foods for in-laws to be could not be ignored or substituted with any other. So on the day of this important visit, Munyao's homestead was buzzing with women cooking and preparing special foods for the in-laws. Mutisya's people arrived at the agreed time and on their arrival were greeted and welcomed by Kanini's uncle, Mzee Kitema. They were ushered into a specially prepared room where they were served with all the delicacies.

After they had eaten, they all got ready for the discussion. Customarily, the actual father and mother of both the suitor and the girl do not participate during the dowry negotiatons, although they must be there. Each side chooses their spokesmen, usually their very closest friends, whilst close relatives of both the boy and the girl just sit back and listen. Mutisya's father, Pastor Paul Kyalo, had chosen his childhood friend, to speak on his behalf.

'I do not really know which side I belong to,' began Mzee Ngumbi. 'The reason why I say this is because our late brother Munyao was a very good friend of mine and I would be more than honoured to speak on his behalf. Yet here I am, speaking on the side of our brother, Kyalo. This, I think, is a good sign, and as the saying goes, "when a goat gives birth to twins, it breastfeeds both of them," I too will do my best. So without wasting time and mincing words, we elders and friends of Pastor Kyalo are here today to know the home from which our son, Mutisya, wants to get a wife. We are interested in your daughter's hand, and in the proper Kikamba way, *twoka kuvanda ikonge*, and by so doing we have brought with us something little to offer to you as a token of our good intention.'

Mzee Ngumbi then produced a purse from his inside coat pocket and pulled out ten thousand Kenya shillings, new banknotes. He gave it to Mzee Kasyoki, the chosen spokesman on behalf of Kanini's family. As tradition expects, he asked him to count it. This was done loud enough for everyone to hear. After the counting, Mzee Kasyoki put the money on the table and made a short speech.

'We are very grateful to you parents of Mutisya and we really appreciate your gesture. We do not mean to imply that what you have given to us is not enough to allow you *kuvanda ikonge* (in Kambaland one had to plant sisal plants to mark the boundary of one's land so as to prevent trespass. The piece of property where one planted a sisal became their personal property and in this case, Mutisya's family had declared Kanini their personal property by paying some dowry), however, you Mzee Ngumbi, know the proverb that *Uivena kana kavyu nomuvaka ukanenge muli.* As you take away our daughter, so you must give us a substitute, although there is nothing that can equal our daughter. Just as you must take a knife away from a child because it is dangerous, you must give the child a stick instead, although the stick is not as sharp as the knife. So, as you are prepared to take away our daughter, you must give us a substitute, although the substitute will not be as good as our daughter.'

Mutisya's people asked to be allowed time to go out to consult each other. It only took them a few minutes and then they came back in the house.

'True to the words of that proverb, Mzee Kasyoki,' Mzee Ngumbi said, 'we have another five thousand shillings to add as *muti*.' Mzee Ngumbi handed Mzee Kasyoki another purse containing the money. Both sides were happy with the negotiations, and as a sign of goodwill, both parties embraced one another. The guests were again served with soft drinks and more food. Before the parties left the room, it was agreed that Mutisya and Kanini could go ahead with their wedding arrangements. It was also agreed that the wedding could take place as soon as possible. The only important function that remained and which could be done any time was the *kunengane mwiitu* the last ceremony to get the girl. The rest of the dowry which Mutisya's father said he would pay, would follow after the wedding. Pastor Paul Kyalo was a very rich man, and Mutisya being his only son, he felt that he really should pay the dowry and more for a girl of Kanini's good reputation. She would be the perfect daughter-in-law. It was late in the evening when the two parties parted on very amicable terms.

After the *kunengane mwiitu*, a ceremony closer to a bridal shower which involved among other things the slaughtering of a particularly big, fat lamb for Kanini's clan, everything else was quick and easy. Mzee Kitema, Kanini's paternal uncle on behalf of his late brother, Mzee Munyao, blessed Kanini and declared that Kanini could marry Mutisya and bear him sons and daughters. There could not have been a better way of sending Kanini off than with these fatherly blessings.

CHAPTER
5

◆ ◆ ◆ ◆

Saturday August 20th, 1977 was no ordinary day for Kanini and Mutisya, for on that day they exchanged their marriage vows. The church organ was playing the wedding march. Mutisya and his best man were already in the church awaiting the arrival of the bride. Slowly, with her uncle holding her hand, Kanini walked up the aisle, led by two flower girls and two page boys, while the maids of honour and uniformed officers in their red tunics followed. When she got to the altar, the organist stopped and the priest began the ceremony.

'Dear brethren,' the priest's voice vibrated and filled the church, 'we are gathered here today to witness to the joining in holy matrimony of these two children. Therefore, if anyone has any reason as to why these two should not be joined together as husband and wife, let them speak now or forever hold their peace.' There followed a tense silence. 'Then,' the priest continued, 'there being no objection to the marriage, I will proceed.'

Kanini could almost recite the marriage creed by heart; she had practised so often over the previous few days. 'I, – Pamela Kanini, take thee, James Mutisya, to be my legally wedded husband, to love, to cherish and to hold, for better, for worse, for richer, for poorer, in sickness or in health, till death do us part.'

After Mutisya had also taken the vows, it was time for them to exchange their wedding rings. Mutisya's best man, Major Ethuro, first gave Mutisya Kanini's ring, and the priest guided him in what to say. 'With this ring, I thee wed,' he repeated as he slowly put the thin gold ring on Kanini's ring finger. Kanini took the same vows as Mutisya and she placed the wedding ring on his ring finger. A wild cry of excitement swept through the church as the priest pronounced them, 'husband and wife'. She was now Mrs Pamela Kanini Mutisya.

It had been a very beautiful and colourful wedding. Mutisya's fellow officers, dressed in the red tunics of the ceremonial dress, formed a guard of honour with their shiny swords outside the church for the bridal party to pass through. They clapped their swords together as a sign of congratulations to the newly-weds.

The memories of those wonderful six days together before Mutisya left for Rhodesia remained in Kanini's mind like a sweet dream. Mutisya had been a passionate lover, completely devoted to his new wife, and with all his charm and experience in romance had roused the rather inexperienced Kanini. Major Mutisya had been given married quarters at Nanyuki, where he was based: a lovely mansion, with a beautiful and well-kept compound. They put all their wedding presents in that house and Kanini lovingly arranged and rearranged them. Everything was so new and exciting that even everyday chores were done with smiles and laughter. Mutisya and Kanini were both young and too much in love to care about what was happening outside the four walls of their house.

All too soon, however, came the parting. The night before Mutisya was to leave, neither of them really slept. Over and over again they said all the loving things that many other lovers in their situation before them had said.

'Pam, *muka wakwa*, I'll always love you. I will be faithful to you... you mean the whole world to me! I will always, always write to you, my darling,' Jim promised.

'Jim, promise me you will never stop loving me?' Pam looked up in his eyes as tears streamed down her cheeks.

'Pam, I swear I will love you forever. You are my wife. You are part of my own flesh and life now. I will love you forever!'

The loving words were whispered over and over again, till dawn. Morning finally came and neither of them was able to eat the breakfast Kanini had prepared. They sat close together, and a nervous silence fell in the room until at last a Land Rover arrived to take them to the airport. Kanini was to accompany Mutisya to Nairobi where he and others were to board the plane for Rhodesia.

The journey to Nairobi had been almost unbearable for Kanini who struggled to hold back tears as she imagined the horrible things that might happen to Jim. Jim was himself fighting to control his emotions at the thought that he might never see his wife again. Totally caught up in their own thoughts, they were both surprised how soon they arrived at the Jomo Kenyatta International Airport. The plane that was to fly the officers and servicemen to Rhodesia was ready and waiting, and they had to board it immediately. There was scarcely a minute for the last words of love and farewell to be whispered once again by Mutisya to Kanini or by the many other soldiers to their spouses. They were herded on to the carrier.

With tears streaming uncontrollably from her eyes, Kanini slowly got into the Land Rover which was to take her back to Nanyuki. On the way, through a blur of tears, Kanini admired her golden wedding ring. Why did people have to fight each other? To her, it was a waste of precious time, time that should be used in loving and caring for each other. Kanini loved her husband so much that it broke her heart to think that he had gone to a war-torn country, a country that was so involved in a guerilla war. She recalled how he had assured her of his safety.

'Pam, darling,' he had told her, 'we, the peace-keeping forces, will not be at all involved in the actual fighting. We will be there only to see that peace and order are maintained. We will be observers and will be stationed far from the war zone. Our duty will be to monitor the progress of the ceasefire.' Kanini wished she could believe him.

For young Mrs Pam Mutisya, time dragged by, slowly and miserably. Her only comfort was Mutisya's youngest sister, Lucy Ngina, who had come to stay with her. She went to a school in Nanyuki.

'Thank goodness, my in-laws are more of a blessing than a curse to me,' Kanini once observed. She had time and again heard about how in-laws could make life miserable for the wives of their sons, and sisters of the husband could be equally nasty to their brothers' wives. She welcomed the comfort and support Mutisya's family gave her.

After a few weeks of nursing her loneliness, Kanini reported back to work in her new office in Nanyuki. She had got a transfer from the Nairobi branch of the bank, where she had been working before marrying Mutisya, to the Nanyuki's branch. As time went by, she got to know a few people and soon began to feel a little better. Mutisya, being a good letter writer, wrote long, loving letters every week, which boosted her morale. She looked forward to reading them like an excited schoolgirl. Sometimes, when reading his letters expressing his undying love for her, Kanini almost imagined she was talking to her husband rather than just reading his letters.

Although Kanini would occasionally go to the officers' mess and meet with other officers' wives, she had little time for most of them who were simply out to drink and gossip. She knew she was different from them; all her future was built around Mutisya, and she had to try and make the best of it, even during his absence. She knew she must never yield to any kind of temptation which could give anybody cause to talk about her, or even worse, think of her as an unfaithful wife. She was a soldier's wife and as such she had to be tough, unyielding and committed to do whatever her husband wanted. She had to cope with what many women, especially those in civilian life, would not tolerate. Yes, she had to prove she could be a real soldier's wife.

At times when Kanini felt really lonely and missed her husband, she took out their wedding photo albums and went through the pictures, slowly and methodically, admiring and re-living the memories of each one of them. Sometimes, she wished there had been a child waiting to be born. Perhaps this could have made life without Jim more tolerable – taking care of and nursing Jim's baby – a son or a daughter. But alas! There had been no baby. Mutisya had not wanted a family just yet, and he did not want poor Pam to be burdened with the task of bringing up a child alone.

Sometimes her mind would refuse to let her believe Mutisya's assurances in his letters that he was quite safe, that their camp was far from the warring zones and that he was actually having a nice time. She would undergo mental agony, picturing him dead, blown into small fragments of human flesh. '*Oh, dear God, never let it happen!*' She would then sigh aloud, and would feverishly wait for any news. Sometimes she would ring his office, just to talk to anybody who could reassure her of his safety.

During these years of separation from her husband, Kanini enjoyed a happy relationship with her in-laws. They made her feel wanted and loved and this helped her feel secure, even without Jim around. She felt happy that she had made the right decision to marry Mutisya, and knew that she and Jim had only to be together again and life would be perfect.

It was with this feverish anticipation that Kanini had boarded the plane for Rhodesia to join Jim. Kanini's mother, her parents-in-law, various other in-laws, relatives and friends had come to see her off at the Jomo Kenyatta International Airport. At last she had reached Rhodesia and was actually on her way to the camp where she knew Jim would be waiting for her. '*This,*' she thought, '*will be our second honeymoon!*'

They had covered nearly half their journey when gradually the Land Rover lost all its power and came to a standstill.

'What's the problem?' Major Njoroge asked Corporal Kiptanui, the driver.

'I don't know what it is,' Kiptanui replied. For some time Kiptanui tried to start the vehicle, but the engine would not fire at all. It was completely dead.

'Let's push it to the roadside and see what the problem is,' Major Njoroge told the ladies.

The men pushed it a few yards from the road and then Kiptanui opened the bonnet. While Major Njoroge and the driver were busy trying to locate the problem, Pam and Kate had time to admire the country's beautiful scenery. After nearly two hours of struggle, still the vehicle would not start. Night would soon fall. Their only hope was that, being a main road, they would get a lift to a nearby small town from where they could perhaps arrange transport to take them to the camp. Then, just as they were discussing about their next move, they saw the headlights of an approaching vehicle flashing from a distance, as if enquiring whether its occupants could offer any assistance. Njoroge quickly moved near the road and flagged the vehicle down. It stopped a few yards in front of their Land Rover.

'Ah! Thank goodness it's you, Sir!' Major Njoroge said, with relief, as he stood to attention and saluted on recognising an officer of higher rank in the vehicle. Brigadier George Okonkwo was from Nigeria and was the Commanding Officer of the Nigerian troops.

'What's the problem, Major?' he asked Njoroge.

'Sir, the Land Rover just came to a standstill. We've been trying to find out what the problem is, but without luck.' There was a pause as Major Njoroge moved towards his Land Rover. Then he spoke again, 'Ah, Sir! Meet Mrs Pam Mutisya - Lieutenant-Colonel Mutisya's wife, and this is my wife, Kate. They have just arrived from home – we've been to meet them. This is Brigadier Okonkwo, from Nigeria,' he said, turning to Pam and Kate.

'My pleasure to meet you, ladies,' Brigadier Okonkwo said, as he greeted each of them in turn. 'I hope you have not been stuck here for long?'

'Well, not very long. Maybe an hour or so,' replied Kate.

Even with the help of Brigadier Okonkwo, the problem with the Land Rover could not be established.

'I think the problem lies deeper than we think,' said the Brigadier. 'I suggest we tow it to the camp. It's only a couple of miles away. The ladies can come with me in my vehicle and you, Major, can accompany your driver, just in case.'

'Yes, Sir. Thank you, Sir,' replied Major Njoroge, as he saluted the Brigadier.

It was quite dark when at last they got to the camp. They all felt tired and thirsty, and a cold drink in the officers' mess was welcomed by all. After the drink, Njoroge decided to take the two ladies to the married quarters so that they could at least rest a little before dinner. The ladies were standing to go when a waiter approached them and enquired which of them was Mrs Mutisya. Kanini, tired and exhausted after the fraught journey, was also worried and tense about her husband's absence. She had not seen or heard anything about the whereabouts of her husband, or any reason why he had not come to meet her. Although she had not said anything, she felt deep down that there was something wrong.

'I'm Mrs Mutisya,' she told the waiter, anxiously.

'Madam, this letter is for you. Boss left it with me and asked me to give it to you,' said the waiter.

'Thank you very much,' Kanini said as she quickly took the envelope from him.

Kanini hurriedly opened the envelope, her fingers trembling. A single door key fell out. With it was a note which appeared to have been written in a great hurry. Kanini read it through.

'Sorry, Pam. I had to go on an urgent mission. Our married quarters are second on the right. Make yourself at home. I'll see you when I get back.

Yours, Jim.'

Her spirits fell. Even without her husband's note, Kanini would still have found their married quarters; Major Njoroge would have shown her, and in fact he did show her, despite her husband's note telling her where it was.

'We shall call on you in, say, about an hour's time so that we can go and have dinner,' said Major Njoroge kindly, as he opened the door for Kanini. Once inside the house, Kanini poured all the tears that had been burning in her eyes.

'There must be something wrong with Jim! He didn't even say, "Welcome to Rhodesia, Pam" or even that he still loves me, or has missed me and was looking forward to my arrival. He just wrote a note. Just a note! That's all he thinks I'm worth!' Kanini wept until the tears were no more. She was bitterly disappointed, hurt and exhausted from her journey. Suddenly, she looked at the note once again and laughed.

'I think I am misjudging Jim. He must have been in a hurry, when he wrote this note. I know he loves me and cares for me. She felt she must try to understand why Jim had been unable to meet her, but she found it impossible to explain why he had not written a more welcoming, loving letter. She must try and understand… soldier's wife she was and as a soldier's wife she must accept Jim's short note. Kanini could not tell how long she sat down, crying and trying to force bad thoughts about her husband out of her mind.

Then she remembered that the Njoroges were due to pick her up for dinner. Looking at her watch, she realised they could knock on the door any minute. Quickly she pulled herself together, had a quick shower and dressed in a beautiful Kanga outfit. Kanini never wore much make-up, and did not approve of women who did, especially, married ones. All she used was a little cream and powder.

Once contented with her appearance, Kanini made another tour of her new home, while she waited for the Njoroges to arrive. As she walked around, her mind was flooded with questions – questions whose answers she did not know. In fact, in many ways she dreaded knowing their answers. She did not want to think that her husband's inability to meet her was anything other than that he was on official business. One could never tell in a place like this, where land mines were planted everywhere. Such thoughts refused to be pushed aside and, as much as she tried to keep a hold of herself, it was impossible. Pam began to cry again.

'*Well, I suppose I just have to take it in my step and pray that he is all right,*' she told herself loudly, in between sobs, throwing her hands up in a hopeless gesture. Her desperate thoughts were interrupted by a soft knock on the door. After wiping her eyes quickly and checking her face in the mirror, she went to open it.

'*That must be the Njoroges,*' she thought as she opened the door. '*Kate is a lucky girl to have a welcoming husband like Njoroge.*' She unbolted the door and held it ajar.

'Wow! Look at that! You look gorgeous, my dear!' exclaimed Kate, as she admired Kanini's outfit.

'Thanks, Kate. You too look great,' replied Kanini in the same excited tone as she closed the door behind her and put the single key in her purse.

'I just hope your husband turns up soon and sees just how beautiful you look in that outfit,' Kate continued as they got in the Land Rover, showing an obvious admiration for Pam.

'Ah, well, I hope so too...,' replied Kanini. She felt down-hearted and, much as she tried to hide her feelings, her disappointment was obvious, both on her face and in her voice.

They reached the officers' mess and a waiter showed them to the dining room. It was directly opposite the bar as one entered through the main door. This gave them a clear view of who came in and who went out. The food was delicious, but Kanini had no appetite. She sipped a little of the Black Tower wine served with the dinner. It was the bitterest thing that she could ever remember having tasted in her lifetime.

'My whole life is now as bitter as this wine!' she thought sadly.

Mutisya had made everything bitter and sour for her; she would neither forgive nor forget this 'welcome'. Her mind was once again wandering uncontrollably, as she looked at the Njoroges and saw how happy they were. If her kind of life was what she had signed that marriage certificate for, then God forbid; it was the most miserable life one could have on this earth! Not being together with one's husband when one wanted...always putting his duty first... what else was to follow?

Then, a voice cut into her thoughts. Njoroge was speaking; 'Soldiers' wives lead the most unpredictable lives on this earth. They are lucky if they stay together for a couple of months without the husband being posted away, and most likely in the bush! And,' he added, sounding very serious, 'that's why before any soldier marries, he looks for a girl who can be reliable, trustworthy, and strong, in that she can take all the changes that may arise from time to time in her stride - even death... and, of course, she must be beautiful!' he added, looking at his wife.

CHAPTER

6

♦ ♦ ♦ ♦

It was while Kanini was drinking her third glass of wine that Brigadier Okonkwo joined them.

'So, how is everybody?' he greeted them, as he pulled a nearby chair from an unoccupied table. The Nigerian Peace-Keeping Force's camp was not far from the Kenyan one and the troops could visit each other freely.

'We are fine, Sir,' Njoroge replied.

'Has the Lieutenant-Colonel turned up yet, Madam?' he asked, looking straight at Pam.

'Ah, well, not yet,' she said, feeling embarrassed. 'I guess he must still be held up.'

'Well, we all have to put up with sudden changes in plans,' put in Brigadier Okonkwo. 'And especially when one is a soldier's wife you have a lot of unforeseen circumstances to live with; you find that the most ridiculous things happen just when they're least expected!'

Brigadier Okonkwo, being a very experienced officer and commander of the Nigerian Peace-Keeping Troops, had seen a lot. There were frequent parties and dances to boost the morale of both the officers and the servicemen. He knew that most men had made friends with the Rhodesian girls, and it went without saying that some of them had actually become romantically involved. Personally, he had not met Lieutenant-Colonel Mutisya, but all he hoped was that he wasn't one of the merry-go-round fellows. He himself, although very handsome, was a very serious man and had neither the time nor the inclination to form relationships with girls. However, despite his cheerful appearance, Brigadier Okonkwo was a very lonely man. At that particular moment, sitting next to Kanini, he felt even lonelier. One glance at her smiling face and he experienced a pain that was almost too much for him to bear. She looked like Janet! His Janet! The face, body build, complexion, colour of the hair, and the shy smile which exposed a small gap between her white, evenly arranged top teeth. She was Janet all over! God alone knew how much he had loved Janet. How perfect life was when they were together! She had been his whole life and all his hopes.

In those moments, he relived the sad memories he had suppressed for so long. He had always sworn to try and forget these memories, yet never to forget Janet herself. Five painful years had gone by, yet the memories of Janet were as fresh in his mind as if it had all happened the day before. It was two weeks before their marriage. Her wedding dress was already in her wardrobe, awaiting the big day. The wedding ring had been bought and engraved with his own initials and the date of the wedding 'G.O. -26.8.72'. The church rehearsals with the local priest had been well-practised too.

Customarily, a girl getting married was expected to hold a party for her village peer group, a farewell party for those who might not be able to attend the wedding itself. On this day, Okonkwo had gone with Janet to her village and they had enjoyed a perfect day's celebrations. Janet's friends had decorated her with beautiful African ornaments and gowns, as befit a bride to be. They made her dance and they carried her shoulder high while they danced to wedding songs. She looked the perfect African bride.

Okonkwo remembered very well how these friends of Janet had shed tears, tears of both happiness and sorrow. Happiness because she had found a well-respected man to marry her, and sorrow because they were going to miss her company. They sang farewell traditional songs for Janet, who was to leave her girlhood and become a married woman. Then, just before sunset, both Okonkwo and Janet had said their last farewell to all those dear friends, young and old, and had started their journey back to Lagos, which was about one hundred miles away from Janet's village.

They had gone about halfway, when tragedy struck. A tanker with a long trailer lost control, swerved towards them and before Okonkwo knew it, his car had left the road and overturned. He saw and remembered no more. He was unconscious for three days. Janet had died on arrival at the hospital.

Okonkwo vaguely remembered seeing people around him cry whenever he stammered Janet's name. He desperately wanted to know the truth. They hadn't the courage to break the dreadful news to him – at least, not yet. For his sake, they had kept the truth from him until the funeral day, when they could no longer withhold the agonising truth about her.

He cried his heart out like a small baby. He was not even allowed to attend Janet's funeral. The doctors said he was not yet off the danger list and could not leave the hospital.

'Why Janet? Why... my poor Janet!' he wept. 'Without a word of farewell, you are gone, gone beyond my reach, never to come back to me!' he cried, not feeling the physical pain of his injuries, but for his Janet, his dear Janet.

Brigadier Okonkwo was confined to the hospital bed for three months, after which he was discharged and went back to his unit, a disillusioned and self-pitying man. Okonkwo had changed a lot. Life was no longer meaningful to him; he only lived a day at a time and held no hopes for the future. He had hidden the wedding ring, never wanting to see it again, yet treasuring it for its memories of Janet.

It had taken Okonkwo a long time to learn to smile again, to really enjoy and appreciate life. There had been nobody else after Janet, and he never supposed there would ever be anyone to take Janet's place in his heart. Her photograph was placed on his dressing table in his room in the officers' quarters. Every time he looked at it, he became more and more convinced that he would never ever ask another girl to marry him in Janet's place.

And now, sitting next to Pam Mutisya, a total stranger who so closely resembled his Janet, sent a new pang of pain straight into his heart. What upset him even more was that Mrs Mutisya was so miserable because her husband had not turned up. All he wanted to do was get Mutisya and skin him alive for making this poor lady look so unhappy.

'Have you tried to call on the radio to trace his whereabouts, Major?' Brigadier Okonkwo asked Major Njoroge.

'Yes, Sir, I have and the response I got was that he had left the operation area and was heading for the Headquarters,' Major Njoroge answered.

'Did they tell you how long ago that was?'

'Well, quite a while ago, but he was expected to pass through various locations, Sir,' Major Njoroge told the Brigadier, knowing full well that the Brigadier knew he was telling a lie. But he was lying for Pam's sake, hoping that she would believe her husband was delayed on official business.

'He should be coming soon then,' Brigadier Okonkwo said, closing the subject and signalling a passing waiter.

'Another bottle of Black Tower for the ladies, White Cap for the Major and a double gin and tonic for me.'

After another drink, Kanini found herself feeling more comfortable and relaxed. The Brigadier's concern had made her feel a bit better. 'That's the good thing about being associated with these army people,' she thought. They always show concern and respect for their fellow officers' wives, even if they don't know them personally. As soon as they knew you were a fellow officer's wife, you were made to feel completely at home.'

'Jim, muume wakwa,' Kanini thought, *''I love you so much and I do hope that all is well with you, wherever you are, for I long to see you, to be re-united and happy together...'*

Her thoughts were interrupted by Brigadier Okonkwo who spoke directly to her, 'It is so ridiculous how our soldiers, and even officers like ourselves, have grown as slow as the local people here. It's funny; these people here have lost the sense of urgency. One has to have the patience of a judge to wait and see things properly done. Poor ladies! The first lesson for you to learn is to be patient (even with your own husbands) for not keeping time. Nobody seems to be in any hurry here!' The Brigadier said as he looked at Pam.

So the evening went on. Before Kanini knew it, it was midnight. 'Sir,' said Major Njoroge, addressing Brigadier Okonkwo, 'Will you excuse us? I think I ought to take the ladies back now. They must be feeling tired out after their bumpy flight.'

'Ah, yes, of course you should. They must be feeling tired,' added the Brigadier.

That night, Kanini tried to put herself to sleep but she couldn't. She tossed and turned in bed till morning. When she finally got out of bed, it was to answer a knock on the door. 'That might be Jim! Poor Jim, he's been on duty all day and all night, and perhaps he has been travelling all night... he must be feeling pretty tired and awful,' she thought, as she half ran to open the door.

As she opened it, she was disappointed to find that it was only the mess waiter. He had come to announce that breakfast was ready. 'Thank you, I think I'd rather skip breakfast and sleep. I will, however, be up for lunch,' she told the waiter. Major Njoroge had explained the night before that they had a choice of eating in the mess or making their own meals.

A very dejected Kanini went back to bed, not to sleep but to quietly think things out. Falling asleep, even after taking sleeping pills was impossible for Pam. Her mind was a whirl of thoughts. She found it difficult to think clearly. However, she knew one thing: she wanted to believe that Jim was somewhere safe and that before long, he would come to her, take her tenderly in his loving arms and whisper all the sweet things she longed to hear him say.

When she next looked at her watch it was half past twelve. Soon there would be another knock on the door. The waiter would soon be there to announce that lunch was ready. With a heavy sigh, she dressed herself in a long Kanga outfit and tied on a matching headscarf, she was no longer a girl to be overdressed. A few minutes later, Kanini found herself sitting comfortably in the mess, sipping a cold drink; she was feeling thirsty after taking wine the previous night. As she drank, she wondered how long it would take her to get used to what already seemed to be a lonely and boring life. Lost in these thoughts, she watched a variety of military vehicles pass by when Brigadier Okonkwo joined her and offered to buy her a drink.

'How do you like this place, Madam? Any comparison with Kenya's beautiful climate and scenery?' he asked her.

'Well, it's not a bad place at all, though of course it does not compare with my own country's climate – Kenya's is superb!' she replied.

'I know. I myself have been to Kenya once and I must say your country is beautiful. Kenya is simply awesome as a country, and the people are also very friendly, I must say.' Soon lunch was served. Kanini was feeling hungry and she ate quite well.

After lunch the two sat outside under a big sunshade. Kanini felt comfortable in the company of the Nigerian Brigadier. He was a charming person to talk to and Kanini found herself freely talking to him about herself and her husband, Mutisya. In return, Brigadier Okonkwo had told her all about himself.

'It is very, very strange how people, even hundreds or thousands of miles apart, and from totally different countries can resemble each other. It really surprises me,' he had suddenly said to Kanini. 'Why do you say that?' Kanini asked him.

Okonkwo tried to avoid looking at Kanini and didn't answer her question. It was as though he wished he'd never said anything. He went suddenly quiet and seemed unhappy and distracted. He was trying to visualise the image of his beloved Janet. Kanini, still looking at him, thought she noticed him making a face as if he was in pain.

'What's wrong, Brigadier?' she asked him in a worried tone. 'Oh ... er ... ' he sighed, with a forced smile, 'I'm sorry. I... er... I was just thinking... I was thinking about home. I guess I'm feeling homesick,' he lied.

'Have you been out here for long then?' she asked him sympathetically.

'Well, as a matter of fact, I have been here for the last three years which is pretty long enough to make even a man feel homesick, although of course we soldiers are not supposed to feel that way... but then, there it is... ' he added, with a hopeless gesture that left Kanini thinking that the man felt more miserable than he looked or had admitted to. As the two sat talking, Kanini told Brigadier Okonkwo about her home and her hasty marriage to Mutisya because he had been posted to Rhodesia. 'We only knew each other for a short time, although in fact our parents knew each other very well. Our married life together lasted only for a few days, and then he came here. Since then, we both have lived for each other's letters and memories.

'Oh, I'm sorry about that. War is no good for anyone. It makes life difficult and many, many couples never even see each other again, after the soldier husbands go to war. It's a real pity and a sad affair to think how many young widows there are in this world often with young fatherless children. God alone knows how many of us have seen and born tragedies like those born by the biblical Job during his life on earth,' Brigadier Okonkwo told Kanini. A waiter passed by and Brigadier Okonkwo called him. 'Bring a well-chilled bottle of Black Tower for Madam, and for me a gin and tonic on the rocks.'

'My husband owes you a lot for all this kindness, Brigadier Okonkwo.'

'Do call me George, and allow me the pleasure of calling you Pam.'

Kanini was relaxed and comfortable talking to Brigadier Okonkwo but even with Brigadier Okonkwo's friendly company, her spirits began to dampen again. The thought that Mutisya would not come and that she might have to wait for another day or even two before he turned up for their reunion filled her eyes with unshed tears. She had looked forward to their reunion so much that his absence hurt more than she could bear.

Brigadier Okonkwo noticed the misery on Kanini's face but he knew he could do nothing to relieve it. Only the arrival of Mutisya, her husband, would make her truly happy.

'He's a very lucky guy,' Okonkwo thought with some bitterness. *'Some guys are blessed, yet they are too blind to see or appreciate their blessings. What an inconsiderate fellow this Mutisya must be, not even to have bothered to radio the mess for news of his wife's arrival and to let her know his whereabouts. This is a very bad show on his part as a senior military officer!'*

Okonkwo realised that the best he could do for Kanini was to stay a little while longer with her. He suggested to her that they go for a drive to break the boredom of sitting around waiting all day. He could get one of the Land Rovers and show her the area and maybe go to the nearest town.

'That is, if you are not feeling very tired or bored with my company... ' he added as an afterthought.

'You are very kind George and you are a really good companion; take it from me, I really am glad that you came. I'd love to have a look around.'

Kanini had thought a drive would distract her mind from her worries about Mutisya, but even though she enjoyed the ride with George and tried hard to take an interest in the places they passed through, she still felt very distraught. She bitterly thought about how, after they got back to the camp, Brigadier Okonkwo would drop her at her new quarters and she would be all alone again. She was now thinking negatively rather than positively about the possibility of finding Mutisya at home when they got back.

Just as she had anticipated, when they got back long after seven o'clock, there were no signs of her husband. Brigadier Okonkwo suggested that they have supper in the mess before he took her back to her house but Kanini politely declined.

'You cannot sleep hungry,' he told her when she refused to have dinner with him.

'But strictly speaking, I'm not feeling hungry at all. I haven't got any appetite,' she replied.

'I know that, and I understand why, but still I insist on you eating something – no matter how little; you should have something. And that,' he added jokingly, 'is an order, Madam!'

Kanini was not one to argue by nature and she found herself obeying the 'order'. They went in the dining room and sat at the same table they had shared with the Njoroges the previous night. Only this time, the Njoroges were not there. Although neither of them mentioned the Njoroges, Kanini thought enviously, not for the first time, of Kate. What a lucky girl she was to have married a good and considerate man like Njoroge.

Brigadier Okonkwo, studying Kanini quietly, knew exactly what was on her mind but he did not show it. While they waited for dinner to be served, he persuaded her to take some wine.

'It will do you good and may even give you some appetite,' he told her, after she had protested and refused to have anything other than a glass of fruit juice. Eventually, she agreed to have some wine.

It soon became obvious as they sat there, that Kanini's eyes were constantly fixed on the entrance door. She kept hoping Mutisya would show up and that the first place he might come to would be the mess.

Thank goodness, Brigadier Okonkwo thought that he was not the type of man who went out to have fun with beautiful girls such as Kanini, whether she was married or not. He was glad to reflect that this lady seated opposite him was a decent girl, who was without a doubt whole-heartedly in love with her soldier husband. This knowledge, and the fact that Kanini did not concentrate on what the Brigadier was telling her, did not annoy him at all; in fact he respected and admired her feelings. As the two sat eating their dinner, Kanini could not stop fear from creeping into her mind, in a few hours' time she would leave the company of Brigadier Okonkwo and would be tossing in her big bed, alone and cold, both mentally and bodily. This thought brought back to her the memory of a friend back in Nanyuki who once told her that when she felt lonely and was not sure of where her husband was, she sang a special song. She believed that this song would bring him home. Kanini could remember the words of that song well:

'Out in a cold world and far away from home,
Somebody's boy is wandering alone,
No one is to guide him and set his foot a straight,
Somebody's boy is wandering alone.

Bring back my boy, my wandering boy,
Far, far away, wherever he may be,
Tell him his wife will set his foot a straight and
After all, she is waiting for him. '

Kanini finished her food and Brigadier Okonkwo ordered another glass of wine for her. 'No more please, George. I think I have had enough. In fact, if you don't mind, I think I would like to go home and sleep,' she told him.

'All right then. Let's have some coffee and then I can drop you off,' he suggested.

'I'd like coffee, thank you,' she agreed.

Brigadier Okonkwo beckoned a passing waiter and ordered

two coffees. As they drank their coffee in silence, Kanini drew back again into her lonely shell and began to sing another old hit which she used to sing with her friends during her school days, she sang it in her heart.

'My bonny lies over the ocean,
My bonny lies over the sea,
My bonny lies over the ocean,
Oh, bring back my bonny to me.

Bring back, bring back,
Oh, bring back my bonny to me.

Last night as I lay on my pillow,
Last night as I lay on my bed,
Last night as I lay on my pillow,
I dreamt that my bonny was dead.

Bring back, bring back,
Oh, bring back my bonny to me.

The wind has blown over the ocean,
The wind has blown over the sea,
The wind has blown over the ocean,
And brought back my bonny to me.

As soon as she'd finished the song, Kanini felt embarrassed, as if she'd sang it aloud and Brigadier Okonkwo had been listening to her. However, Brigadier Okonkwo was busy looking through a local newspaper and did not notice Kanini's uneasiness. Just then, three officers of lower rank sat down with their drinks at a table nearby. They were talking about another officer, who had taken away a girlfriend belonging to one of them. Kanini could not help but eavesdrop on their conversation.

'*Huyu mtu bwana,*' the complainant said, '*amezidi kabisa!* I'm not afraid – he could be a general for all I care – but the fact remains that he's a real crook! I mean, let's face it,' he'd continued even more loudly and with more bitterness in his voice, 'I'm a very junior officer, but the man had no right to snatch her from me. I gather they went to the capital together... her home town.'

Kanini had almost had enough of listening to the complaints from the young officer, when suddenly she overheard the worst bit of the story, and her heart nearly stopped beating.

'I hear he is a married man, married to a very beautiful wife,' the officer started, 'and, poor thing, she comes all the way from home to be with him and the man is away having a great time with a girl he has snatched from his junior officer. I wonder what excuses he will have to tell his wife? What kept him away for two or so days?'

'Official duties, what else!' replied another.

'I could be unfaithful to my wife but I think I would be decent and considerate enough to actually meet my own wife!' said the complaining officer.

'Sssshhhhh...You had better be quiet, or you will be... here comes the "officer and the gentleman" himself!'

'Aah... who cares!' grumbled the complainant.

On hearing the warning signal, Kanini's eyes turned involuntarily towards the door. There was Jim, her husband, followed by Major Njoroge and his wife, Kate.

'He is quite smart, eh! He's got company to cover him up. A nice trick, isn't it? Very, very clever and it's quite smart for him.

Kanini did not wait to hear anymore. Like lightning, she stood up. Brigadier Okonkwo looked up from the paper he was reading, thinking that Kanini had finished her coffee and was ready to go.

'Here comes my husband at last!' Kanini announced. Ignoring all the allegations she had just heard, and which she had rightly connected with her husband. She crossed the floor, half shouting his name. Mutisya also saw her and he too ran across the room. Disregarding all that were present, they hugged each other. If Kanini had thought that her husband had not missed her or did not love her, she now was proved wrong. He embraced her as she had longed to be, and for her part she knew she was still very much in love with her soldier husband. Whatever suspicions or doubts she had had, she was not going to show them now— at least, not in the officers' mess and in front of his colleagues, both junior and senior. She was not going to wash her dirty linen in public; she would wait and discuss things later with Jim, when the two were alone, and, of course, she expected an explanation from him for all these allegations. Brigadier Okonkwo looked, speechless, at the two figures – one he admired, the other he despised.

'I'm sorry my Pam! It was rotten luck I was not here to meet you...'

'Oh, that's all right Jim, I understand. I was met by Njoroge, and by the way,' she said, as she led him towards Brigadier Okonkwo, 'come and say hello to the Nigerian officer who has also kept me company.'

'Hello, Sir,' Mutisya greeted Brigadier Okonkwo and stood to attention as he greeted him.

'Hello Lieutenant-Colonel,' replied Brigadier Okonkwo as he offered his hand to Mutisya.

'Thank you very much, Sir, for looking after my wife.'

'Not at all. Why don't we all sit down and have a drink?' Brigadier Okonkwo suggested as he helped pull more chairs up to the table.

A waiter was called and Mutisya ordered drinks. As they drank and talked, Brigadier Okonkwo became convinced that Mutisya had not been away from the camp on official duties, but on a personal matter. To this end, he concluded that a woman must have been involved in his absence. He felt hatred towards him well up in his heart. He had formed a negative opinion of Mutisya's trustworthiness the minute Kanini had introduced them. He sympathised with her and admired the spirit in which she'd taken everything in and now looked radiant, sipping her wine comfortably and happily, sitting very close to Jim. She looked beautiful; a completely different Pam from the dull and unsmiling one he had taken out for a ride a few hours earlier.

Undoubtedly, Mutisya was a handsome and charming man but he looked like he could easily misuse those personal qualities on women when he chose to and turn into a lady-killer or even a playboy. Although Brigadier Okonkwo did not want to condemn Mutisya without knowing the facts, he now guessed that he was the much talked about senior officer who had got temporarily married to local girls.

He had heard some officers in his own camp talk about it. It also occurred to him that Mutisya was actually the much gossiped about senior officer who ran away with his junior officer's girlfriend. Christ Almighty! He must be the one! Brigadier Okonkwo could not imagine what such a beautiful innocent young girl as Kanini had ever seen in him. Perhaps it had been physical attraction; Mutisya was certainly good-looking.

Kate, on the other hand, was happy for her friend, Pam. At last Jim had shown up in one piece. *'He is a real charmer! Little wonder Pam is still head over heels in love with him,'* Kate thought.

While everybody else formed their own opinion about Lieutenant-Colonel Jim Mutisya, Kanini was thinking about the few days they had spent honeymooning after their hurried wedding. Sweet memories, and worthy of treasure. *'Thank heavens I feel like a bride again, even after all those long months of separation...'*

Brigadier Okonkwo interrupted her thoughts as he stood up and announced his departure. 'Well, well, now that the Lieutenant-Colonel is here, I wish to fall out and then he can take over the command,' he said, jokingly, forcing a smile. Everyone stood up to say goodnight to him. The two officers stood to attention, as is expected of a junior officer when a senior officer comes in or goes out.

'Once again, thank you very much, Sir, for keeping my wife company. I really appreciate all you have done, Sir,' said Jim. 'Oh, my pleasure. It was my duty to see to it that the lady was comfortable, Jim,' Brigadier Okonkwo replied, calling Mutisya by his first name.

Soon after the Nigerian Commander had gone, the party broke up. Jim, feeling drunk and sleepy, decided to take his tired-looking wife home for an early night. Major Njoroge and Kate also wanted to retire early.

Once alone in their married quarters, Jim showed his wife that he still loved and cared for her more than ever. For reasons which even she herself did not understand, Kanini felt he was overdoing everything rather, as if he had a guilty conscience he wanted to conceal. Strangely, she felt uncomfortable being alone with Jim. He looked like a stranger and talked of unfamiliar things to her. She wondered why tonight, of all the nights, she could not feel happy to be together with her husband after so many long and lonely months of separation. Hadn't she longed day in, day out, for their re-union, a moment like this when they would be together and alone?

'You haven't changed a bit, my beloved *kiveti*. You look as beautiful as ever. No wonder the Brigadier could not help but keep you company...' Those words, Jim regretted them as soon as they were out of his mouth.

Kanini felt annoyance and bitterness well up within her. 'How could you possibly say that, Jim? Instead of appreciating all the Brigadier did for you? I mean, seeing to it that I, your wife, was comfortable and not lonely, why do you say something so unpleasant? How could you be so ungrateful! You...'

'Hold your horses, my dear wife. You don't think that a lonely Brigadier would waste his time keeping a comrade's wife busy all for nothing? You think he was just being kind, eh! You know, being 'a gentleman and an officer', I'm sure the "kind" Brigadier was only too happy to be of some use to a beautiful woman like you.'

'Jim! That's so ungrateful and very, very unkind of you to say such things against the Brigadier. He was only trying to make me feel at home and...'

'I know all that. Take it or leave it! But I must warn you, my dear wife, you have a lot to learn about these army officers and soon my dear, very soon, you will put the "kind" Brigadier where he belongs and stop thinking the best of him.'

Kanini was horrified to hear such abusive words from her husband's mouth. She had not answered him. She dared not. This was a completely different man from the one she knew. The Mutisya she had married was no more. He was gone. She was scared with all her soul; she dreaded and regretted her ever coming to Rhodesia, yet this was their very first night together since she had arrived. Could all this be really happening?

CHAPTER

7

◆ ◆ ◆ ◆

Jim Mutisya woke up a very sick man the following day. He had thought that by drinking, he would forget Rosetta and show genuine love to Pam. But instead, he woke up with a king-sized hangover and the memories of the holidays he had spent with Rosetta still fresh on his mind.

'Women! Women! Why ever did God create them? He alone knows, but I think it was a cruel joke!' lamented Mutisya inwardly. *'Why, oh why?'* he asked himself for the umpteenth time as he watched Kanini go to fetch a cold drink for him from the small fridge at the corner of the kitchen. He bitterly recalled some of the loving expressions that Kanini had written to him and how after he had read her letters he had sworn to be faithful to his *Kiveti*, to love only her, always. Then after a short time, he would be introduced to another beautiful woman and then he would forget all about being faithful and loving to his wife. It was always like that; he was weak...yes, that's what he was

It had not taken him very long after his arrival in Rhodesia to find himself involved with a woman. His first affair started during their welcoming party, hosted by the Rhodesians. There, he had met Annie. At first, it appeared like an innocent friendship. Then as the days went by and their meetings became more regular, the whole innocent friendship turned into a full-blown affair, whose results saw Annie carrying an illegitimate baby and losing her job as a receptionist in one of the big hotels in Rhodesia. Mutisya sincerely regretted the part he had played in ruining Annie's life. The innocent girl had not even known that he was married and would never marry her.

Annie was soon forgotten and the vacuum she had created in Jim's heart was soon filled. Rosetta was a fiancée to a Major Michael Kajube, a Rhodesian officer. The Major and his fiancée had met Jim at a dance party organised by the Rhodesian troops as a get-together during the Christmas celebrations. It was love at first sight for Jim and Rosetta, and when they took to the floor to dance they both realised the feeling was mutual. Major Mike, as he was known to his friends, was a cool man and talked only when he thought it necessary. Rosetta was the extreme opposite; she liked talking and socialising, and often got bored whenever she was with Mike.

Rosetta did not have to tell Mutisya about her fiancé but Jim, with his experience of women, knew that the Major was a real bore to Rosetta. Jim found her both very romantic and extremely amusing after she had had a few drinks. She danced beautifully and was a good match for Jim. She, or so Jim thought, was too beautiful and lively for poor Major Mike who, without even noticing that his fiancée was dancing cheek-to-cheek with Jim in a quiet corner, went on chatting with his fellow officers while he sipped his drink.

That dance decided it all; Jim and Rosetta had hit it off like two live wires coming together. Mutisya wanted Rosetta, wanted her madly and without any pity for her sober, good-natured and unsuspecting fiancé. Rosetta, too, was crazy about Jim and thought that she could not live if she didn't see him again, and often.

Mutisya's affair with Rosetta was at its climax when Pam arrived in Rhodesia. He was completely intoxicated by Rosetta's charms. She, in turn, had found Jim very handsome, exciting to be with, and not as naive about love as her fiancé, Major Mike. Jim was totally hooked on her; however, he was clear about one thing – he could not risk another serious scandal like Annie's, especially not with Pam's arrival in Rhodesia. Besides, there was Major Mike, innocently engaged to her; there was no way he was going to leave Pam for Rosetta, or have Mike break off his engagement with her, for that matter. He knew he had got himself in deep waters and he had only himself to blame. He had to get himself out of this mess, despite everything he had promised Rosetta. He knew, of course, that several officers knew about this affair but it didn't worry him very much. 'They too are men and could have easily fallen into the trap of a beautiful woman...,' he told himself.

Now Kanini, his beloved wife, was here in Rhodesia. Right in this house. It wasn't fun anymore. People all around him were getting hurt and he was trapped by his own guilt. He recalled Rosetta's reaction on hearing that Pam had arrived.

'Well, Jim: she had said, 'Pam is here now. She is, of course, your wife and I hate her! I hate her for coming to interfere with you... but tell me Jim, why did you ever marry her so hastily? What was the hurry for? Surely you can divorce her as quickly as that, can't you Jim?'

Jim had almost lost his temper with Rosetta, but then he remembered that he had asked himself that same question many, many times whenever he was in Rosetter's arms. Rosetta had just reminded him of it once again. He was not at all sure of the answer.

'Youth, my darling Rosetta,' he had replied reluctantly. 'We were both young and so much in love... infatuated beyond our control. I guess that's what it was. But then... oh, never mind.

There was silence for a moment, then Jim continued, 'If I'm very honest with you Rosetta, I loved and I still love my wife. Somewhere, somehow in my heart of hearts I still love her, and sometimes I wonder what she has ever done to deserve me, honestly Rosetta.'

Rosetta, feeling hurt and not wanting to create a scene, had moved closer to Jim and had kissed him on the lips. Jim pulled her to himself and kissed her violently.

'Breakfast is ready, Jim,' Kanini announced, not knowing that she had interrupted her husband's daydreams about his girlfriend.

When he woke up that morning, Jim had promised himself that he would be the loving, sweet husband of old for his wife. 'Listen, Pam,' he said, 'I'm terribly sorry for not being able to meet you when you arrived. Do forgive me, will you, honey? You know how it is with this kind of work – being pushed around by the bosses and made to do all the travelling and then report back the findings on the ceasefire, and so on. It's not fair, but what can I do? Pam, you do realise it wasn't my wish to be away on your arrival here, don't you, my dear?'

'I do, of course. For you it is duty first and questions or excuses later! I know that is your motto in the forces, so I assure you, Jim, I understand,' Pam answered him with a light heart.

'Thank goodness, that Nigerian brigadier was around to take care of you, my dear. And,' he said, after a pause, 'Pam, I'm sorry I said those things about him last night. I think I was drunk.'

'Oh Jim, I can assure you he was a real gentleman. He did all he could to make me feel happy and welcome,' said Pam, and for a brief moment she reflected in her mind how handsome George looked.

'Pam,' Jim broke in, disrupting her thoughts, 'I want to take you out and show you around this place. Get yourself ready while I go and get a Land Rover. I will be back in a short while,' he told her, as he finished his breakfast.

After he left, Pam had time to follow through her own thoughts. *'Maybe it is true that when a man is away from his wife, he needs a girlfriend to sustain him, and maybe I should forgive him if he has been having an affair with one. But then,'* her thoughts raced on, *'the question of them being away from their wives does not always arise because, men being what they are, they're just as likely to have girlfriends, even under their wives very noses. Men are beasts!'* She recalled some women telling her exactly this some time ago back in Nanyuki. It reminded Pam of a discussion between herself and an old friend. This girl, Sada, was married to an officer who had been sent to the United States on a military course for two years. After some time of being alone, Sada started a love affair. When Pam tried to ask her about the affair, she had defended her actions.

'Listen, my dear Pam, would you tell me in simple language why I should not have a good time while my husband is away? Look, I know for sure, that my dear husband,' she used the words sarcastically, 'has a girlfriend himself – a black American or a white one, for that matter – but that does not bother me because I know it is typical of most men to have affairs outside their marriage. And men don't have to be hundreds or thousands of miles away from their wives to have an affair; that, Pam, goes for your husband as well as mine. They are not angels, and if you think your Jim is an angel, my dear, you may one day get a shock that will stun you forever.'

Her confession certainly shocked Pam to the bottom of her heart. She protested, 'Sada, my dear, you shock me! I can hardly believe or agree with you. My belief is that if somebody loves another and they decide to be joined together in holy matrimony as husband and wife, then one should stick to the other partner, whether they stay far apart or not. The marriage vows are very sacred and cannot be broken or abused. For me, there can never be another man in my life but Jim.'

Sada laughed. 'My dear Pam, I don't want to draw you into anything you disapprove of! I think you are a very naive, faithful wife and I must admit I rather admire your character. But all the same, my dear, I very much doubt whether your Jim will be one tenth as faithful and loyal to you as you are to him. One thing I do know for sure is that men are not as enduring as women. All of them, they are all unfaithful! And, my dear, just remember, if they can be unfaithful when at home, then what about when they are so far away from home?'

Pam, feeling annoyed with Sada, introduced another topic. She did not know that Sada was right; she was such a naive woman that she couldn't picture Jim having fun with any other woman but her, just as she could not picture herself with any other man but Jim.

Her conversation with Sada had been a long time ago. But that morning, in the small kitchen in Rhodesia, miles and miles away from Nanyuki, she was no longer so sure that she felt the same. She bitterly relived that conversation between herself and Sada. The suspicions, doubts and worries of the past few days were now turning round and round in her small head. If only she could now see Sada and talk to her, tell her that she now believed every word that she had said, that all men, including Jim, were beasts, wanton beasts who deserved no respect – certainly not from their faithful wives!

Pam did not realise that she had spent such a long time washing the few dishes. Jim would soon be back to take her for that long drive. She quickly dressed herself for the *safari*, taking every care to look attractive. She must look cheerful, charming and loving. She must show Jim that she was the same beautiful, smart Pam he had once married. She must shut out all the memories of last night, assume that he was drunk and that he hadn't really meant a word of what he had said. It would be better to give him the benefit of doubt. Tonight, she was prepared to make her peace with Jim and start life all over again.

In the midst of her thoughts, Pam heard the roaring engine of a Land Rover and quickly went to open the door. She stood there by the door, expectant and welcoming. The smell of opium perfume brushed Pam's nostrils as Jim came in, kissing her on her cheek.

'Oh, I'm sorry, Pam. I got held up. Did I keep you waiting long, dear?' Mutisya asked her almost breathlessly.

'Oh yeah, Jim I can see that. You don't need to explain who held you up!'

'What exactly do you mean Pam? What can you see that makes you think that I don't have to explain anything and that you know it all?' Mutisya snapped at her. 'I say Pam, what's got into your small head? Did the Brigadier tell you to be rude to your husband and not to respect him anymore?' he finished lamely.

'Now, wait a minute Jim, and stop yelling at me. Why on earth do you keep on smearing an innocent person with your unspeakable accusations? Jim, you don't have to make George the scapegoat. Please let this be the last time you involve him in our misunderstandings,' she paused, and then continued, 'tell me, Jim, how did you get the smell of opium perfume on you?'

Embarrassed and completely lost for words at the bluntness of her question, he was like a man caught red-handed, 'Er, Pam, my dear, that... er... the explanation is simple. You see, I was looking for the sweetest smelling perfume for you and the stupid shopkeeper kept on spraying every perfume I pointed to. You see, Pam, it was as simple as that. Now, can we go for the drive, my dear?'

'And where is the perfume, Jim?'

'Oh... I... er... I couldn't quite find the kind of smell I wanted and, quite frankly, I think this opium is too strong for my liking. I mean, I wouldn't like my wife wearing it. It smells too much, and so I... er... decided to... ' his voice trailed off.

'Decided not to buy it,' she finished the sentence for him. 'Yes, that's right Pam... yeah.'

Pam did not want to start an argument with Jim, but she was not going to pretend that all was well and go for a drive with him as if nothing had happened. What was happening? Jim was now a total stranger to her. This Jim had absolutely nothing in common with the handsome, considerate, sympathetic, loving man she had married. The Jim she now saw was ugly and grotesque, inconsiderate, cold and hard.

'Hey, Pam. What are you waiting for? Let's go, or don't you want to go?'

At that particular moment she was thinking, *'Why, oh why has he changed so much? It is obvious he's been seeing another woman, and from his behaviour, he's certainly in love with her.'* Her pride had been hurt beyond repair; she could not bear to be with him, let alone go for a drive with him as if nothing had happened.

'Jim,' she said, as tears began streaming down her cheeks, 'I don't think I want to go for that drive after all. I can't bear it Jim!' She ran to their bedroom and dropped on the bed.

Jim followed her into the bedroom and tried to plead with her, but to his utter astonishment Pam was not moved by his pleas. She lay there, sobbing on the bed. She felt so hurt that she could not find the words to speak to him. The turn events had taken in such a short time since she arrived in Rhodesia frightened her; she felt she would do almost anything just to get on a plane and go back home. She regretted, for the hundredth time, having come to Rhodesia to join her husband. She had little doubt now that Jim was a totally changed man – a heartless brute was the best description of him. She was determined she was not going to give in to his unworthy, cajoling, sweet nothings and pretend that she would forgive and forget.

Jim lost his temper once he realised that his wife was not going to be easy to convince of his 'innocence'. He had never imagined his Pam not melting in his arms, as she used to. But still, he knew deep down that his anger was because he was guilty, and that guilt pricked him like a thorn in his heart. Blaming and yet not blaming himself for the treatment he was now receiving from his one-time beloved sweetheart, he said, 'Very well, Pam, if you choose to keep quiet then I'll go and look for someone to talk to. I don't want to stay with somebody who will not talk to me!'

'Talk? Talk about what?' Pam found herself saying. 'I know you don't love me anymore. You have no need for me. You have got the woman you love and want. I wish as much as you do that I had never come at all! My good intentions in coming to be with you are your regrets; for it seems by coming I interfered with your tête-à-tête romance! Why, in decency's name; may I ask you Jim, why did you want me to come? Did you just want to embarrass and humiliate me?'

There was a long silence. Finally Jim, feeling overwhelmingly guilty and unable to refute Pam's accusations, completely unable to meet her eyes, got up and went out. He got into the Land Rover but could not bring himself to drive away.

'*Mwana wa kiveti*,' he said to himself, '*you are in a real mess ... a real mess and you deserve a lot worse than what you are getting from your wife. You got yourself in this mess and you have only yourself to blame.*'

Jim did not know how long he sat in the Land Rover, but by the time he gathered his thoughts together and went back to the house, he could tell it was lunch time. Kanini, being the good natured girl she was, she had finally got up and seeing her husband still sitting in the Land Rover had decided to prepare lunch, rather than go to eat in the mess. When Jim walked in the house, Pam was still in the kitchen. She was wiping the cooker. She had put the food on the table ready for serving. On hearing the door open and Jim entering, she stopped cleaning the gas cooker and went straight in the sitting-room to join him. Lunch was eaten in dead silence, save for the soft music coming from the stereo cassette.

In silence Jim suffered his guilt. On looking at his beautiful Pam, he couldn't help but feel very embarrassed, upset and really angry with himself. Then suddenly, he moved over and sat next to her. He put his arm around her waist. 'Pam, my dear wife,' he began gently, 'I am really sorry. I know I have behaved atrociously and you have not known any happiness since you arrived here. Your dreams of the happiness you were looking forward to when we met again after such a long separation have turned to cold ashes. I am really sorry, Pam. Honey, please forgive me! Forgive my wickedness and weakness. I swear I'm going to completely amend my ways, from now on. Will you, Pam, please... ?'

When these words came from Jim's own mouth, Pam did not know whether to love him or hate him more. To forgive

... yes, she could try and forgive him, but to forget... ah... she couldn't! No matter how hard she tried, that was not possible.

Anxious for her reply, Jim drew closer to Pam and looked her straight in the eye, begging for forgiveness. 'Pam, say you have forgiven me!' he whispered in her ear.

Kanini, by nature, was not a woman to cry in front of a man, especially her husband, but she felt tears flowing uncontrollably from her eyes. She pressed her tear-wet cheek against Mutisya's. She could not talk. Mutisya taking advantage of the moment took her in his arms and kissed her hungrily and Pam surrendered herself fully to him.

'Jim,' she asked him faintly, 'do you still love me?'

'Pam, you are my wife, my only wife and I love you. I love you much more than I loved you before our marriage. You are beautiful, Pam, you are...'

When Mutisya said those words to his wife, he meant every word of it; he was really sorry for his misdeeds. He meant to reform after this reconciliation with her and amend his ways, just as he had promised Kanini. He would really try to make her life happy for the rest of their stay there. He swore he would completely forget about Rosetta and stop seeing her.

'I love you too, Jim. You are my husband, and I have forgiven you,' she told him.

'I know I have behaved badly, but I am going to change. Life will be as it used to be back home, I promise you!' he sincerely vowed.

'And Jim? About... about... oh, forget it!' she stammered.

'No, Pam. Don't hesitate. Ask me anything! Anything under this sun!'

'Oh, never mind. It's just that...'

'Pam, honey, I don't mind you not finishing your lunch, but I do mind when you sometimes don't finish your sentence,' Jim said, with a romantic gesture.

'Very well,' Kanini cleared her throat. 'It's about this girl you have been friends with. I…'

'Yes, what about her, Pam?'

'Well, I mean… I…er. .. will you stop going to see her, Jim?'

'Oh come on now, Pam! I have told you things are going to be as they were back home for me and you. By that I mean, my dear, that there will not be anymore *manga-mangering* for me… got it?'

'Oh, Jim! I'm so happy… I…oh, I don't know… '

'And I jolly well mean just that, Pam… no more *zurura zururaring!* I am going to be your old Jim. How about that baby?' he whispered in her ear.'

'I love you, Jim. I have never stopped loving you and now that we are together again, I will love you even more.'

CHAPTER

8

♦ ♦ ♦ ♦

That night when Pam went to sleep, she felt on top of the world. Her Jim had fully come back to her and now she was contented and everything was going to be all right. She would forgive and maybe even forget Jim's past behaviour, close that chapter completely and turn over a new leaf. She would make their stay together in Rhodesia look like a second honeymoon!

The following morning, she woke up feeling happy all over. She prepared a special breakfast for herself and her husband. The air was light and full of laughter as Pam and Jim had their breakfast, giggling and joking as things used to be before Jim came to Rhodesia. And Jim, feeling relieved and happy at having won back his wife's love, gave Pam a quick kiss on her cheek as he got into the waiting Land Rover outside their married quarters and left for work.

'I'm not sure if I will be able to join you for lunch, my dear, so just carry on and don't bother waiting for me,' Mutisya told his wife, as he closed the car door.

Jim had meant well when he spoke those words, but as soon as she was out of his sight, he found himself thinking about Rosetta.

'Damn it! I don't know what to do. I love Rosetta – I want her more than I have ever wanted anything else on this earth. Right now, I can die for her! Her love is all over me ... it's in my blood, my veins - I can feel it! Hell! Why can't a man marry two wives? Oh, hell, hell, hell!'

By the time Mutisya reached his office, he had come to the conclusion that he had to keep both women; one to love and carry on his name, and the other to love and amuse himself with. Rosetta made him feel like a reckless lover. Indeed, that was a large part of her attraction.

When lunchtime came and Mutisya did not appear, Kanini was not bothered. She only hoped that he would at least get something to eat even if it was only the dry ration of tinned beef and biscuits which she knew he detested. After taking her lunch, she lay on the sofa listening to the soft voice of Charlie Pride. She felt romantic; she was in love again – in love with her husband, Jim. It was marvellous to love and be loved again by Jim, because that was all that mattered to her. Under the spell of their new love and the romantic music that acted like a lullaby, Pam fell fast asleep.

It was Jim who woke her up just after five o'clock. 'Hey, sleepy head, wake up! Don't tell me you have been asleep the whole day!'

'Oh dear, time has really flown! I would have gone on sleeping if you hadn't awaken me!' Kanini said, yawning and stretching. 'Anyway, Jim what else could I have been doing, really?' Pam asked lightly, treating the whole conversation as a joke.

'Nothing... nothing in particular, except perhaps bothering to prepare a cup of tea for your husband.'

'Jim,' Pam began, then suddenly she stopped. She feared the

look in his eyes. She sensed danger; something was suddenly wrong. Very wrong. But what – what was wrong? Surely the mere fact that he had found her asleep, not having made his tea could not cause him to lose his temper to that magnitude.

'I live a life which is equivalent to a donkey's: work, work, work, work, and nobody ever appreciates it, not even my dear wife — my dear wife!' he finished, repeating the words sarcastically. Then, in a more authoritative tone he added, 'Get me some whisky and cold water.'

Whatever the matter was, Kanini was not going to ask. She knew him too well. All she knew was that something was very, very wrong, but to ask what it was would be like putting your hand in a beehive. After drawing a number of drinks, Mutisya cleared his throat and declared he was going to bed. He had a bad headache, and did not wish to talk to anybody.

His inability to treat his wife well was, of course, due to his obsession with Rosetta. Mutisya had on reaching his office, made an excuse to go out on urgent business. He had taken his Land Rover and driven himself to Rosetta's flat. He knew it was not the right thing to do, but he could not control his urge to see her.

In Rosetta's flat, he had held her in his arms, and kissed away her meek protests. 'Jim,' she whispered, 'I was hoping that we would behave properly now that your wife is here: you to be the faithful soldier husband and me the faithful soldier's wife-to-be.'

'Listen, Rosetta,' Mutisya spoke to her in a hoarse but firm voice. 'I had thought so too, my darling. But it is not easy to get somebody like you out of my blood system, and just play the faithful soldier husband, answering his wife's calls. Would you like to be the faithful lady-in-waiting for your soldier husband, darling?' In reply, Rosetta kissed him fully on his lips.

'Honey, do you suppose I would? Can you picture me being the lady-in-waiting for anybody else but you?' she said eventually, with a little laugh.

'No, I suppose not. I don't even like to imagine it.'

'But honey, it's going to be difficult for me. Not seeing you every time I want to.

'Difficult? Nothing is going to be difficult. Nothing is going to change! At least, not for me and you. Everything is going to be plain sailing, just like before.'

'But...'

'But what, darling? Don't worry your sweet little head. Leave everything to me; I'll handle the situation, OK? No "buts"! Just pretend everything is normal. You take care of Mike and I'll look after Pam, and you'll see. It'll all work out marvellously.'

Time was not in their favour - it was already late afternoon. 'Damn it!' Mutisya cursed, annoyed to see what the time was. He remembered to have promised Kanini before leaving for work that morning that he would take her out for a drink in town. Pam would have expected him back about four o'clock. He left Rosetta's flat in a jovial mood but it had degenerated into a foul temper by the time he got home. The problems that lay in store for him there were all too real. He knew Pam would ask questions and concluded that the only way to avoid any confrontation with Pam would be to lose his temper. In that respect, his plan had worked but it had not solved any problem.

Mutisya slept the whole night without even waking up for supper. The next morning, he had a quick breakfast and then left for his office. When he came back that evening, with guilt written on his face, he asked Pam to dress up. He would take her out for dinner. The nearest good hotel was about fifty miles away from the camp. All the way, Mutisya had talked and seemed happy. *'A completely different Mutisya from the nagging and abusive one of the previous night,'* Kanini reflected quietly. She had stopped trying to understand her husband; his bad moods seemed to be more frequent than a pregnant woman's.

Their dinner was eaten in almost total silence, save for occasional casual comments about the surroundings and the waiters. Both knew that any conversation was likely to end up on dangerous ground, so they both steered clear. Mutisya knew Pam must be thinking about his behaviour the previous night but did not dare ask her anything. After they had eaten, Mutisya suggested that they drive back and call in at the mess for a drink. It was while on their way back that Mutisya decided to clear the air and, hopefully, his conscience too.

'Pam, my dear, I really don't know what is happening to me. I'm very sorry for what I said last night. I think I behaved disgracefully and said a lot of bad things. I'm very sorry. Believe me, I didn't mean to hurt you. Oh, I guess I was just tired. Please do understand my position. I had been driving all day on a very rough road and had missed a landmine by inches. That's why I lost my temper so easily,' he lied.

'Oh, Jim,' she gasped, 'I'm so sorry! I... I...,' she almost shed a tear when she imagined what would have happened to Jim if he had hit the landmine.

'That's OK, Pam. At least nothing happened. You would think that after all this time I'd be used to living so near to death, but it always shakes one up.' So Mutisya bought Kanini's sympathy with a lie.

With the landmine story dominating their conversation, they reached the campsite. The mess was crowded with officers and a few guests, mainly from other camps. For a brief moment, Mutisya's heart seemed to stop. There, smiling, sitting comfortably and sipping a gin and tonic, was none other than his beloved Rosetta. The moment their eyes met was like two electric wires coming in contact, sparking off a powerful charge. Unfortunately, Kanini had seen the expression on the girl's face: it was clearly not an ordinary look from an ordinary girl to a total stranger. It was an expression that held both meaning and a message. Pam felt the blood drain from her face. She went cold.

Mutisya, somewhat nervously, advanced and introduced his wife to Rosetta. Rosetta was introduced as the fiancée of Mutisya's fellow officer who was sitting with her, Major Mike. After the introductions, the waiter was called for drinks. Kanini was not accustomed to drinking alcohol, and even if she were, the appetite had left her. Everyone, including Rosetta, was drinking alcohol and it sounded slightly odd to them when Pam said that all she wanted was some cold juice.

Mutisya, half acting the gentleman and yet feeling uneasy, had the nerve to attempt to protect his wife. 'My wife was brought up in a very strict Christian family and she does not drink alcohol. She prefers plain water to ginger ale.' That last remark caused laughter to everybody except Pam. To her it was condescending, not funny. Soon after the drinks arrived everybody was busy talking. Casting his eyes towards Pam, Mutisya saw she was busy talking to Rosetta's fiancé, which presented a golden chance for him to whisper a word or two to Rosetta.

'You look edible, my dear! I could devour you!' he whispered to her.

'Thanks, darling. As you can see, he is back.'

'Yes, I had noticed,' replied Mutisya sarcastically, casting an evil eye on Major Mike.

'By the way, tell me – was your wife annoyed with you for being late yesterday?'

With the glass against his lips he replied, 'My wife does not control me, I control her. And honey, I do what I want, when I want to do it. Now, listen to me and listen carefully, it will prove a bit difficult for me to know when and where to meet you. So what you do is ring me in the office when you know he is out of camp. We have to be very careful, honey. You understand?'

Realising that perhaps he had paid too much attention than necessary to Rosetta, Jim moved to the counter and ordered another round. While he was waiting, he strolled round, talking with other officers he knew. By the time he got back to his table, he found several full beer bottles waiting for him. They were the rounds from within the table. Time passed, and Jim enjoyed snatching conversations now and then with Rosetta, ordering more rounds all the time. Pam, exhausted after a long and exacting day, and tired with all the drinking reminded her husband that it was time they went home.

Jim was quite clearly drunk, and the mention of going home irritated him so much that he almost shouted at Pam to shut up. 'For decency's sake, Pam, the night is still young! Nobody is in a hurry to leave, except you. I'm sorry, my dear, you are used to going to bed early, like a baby, but this is not Nanyuki. This is Rhodesia, where people sit and drink and enjoy themselves, without being in a hurry. When in Rome, do as Romans do. Sit still and have another soda.'

At that moment, Pam's eyes met Rosetta's and she noticed a sarcastic smile on the other woman's lips. She felt humiliated but she could do nothing about it. She knew Jim was just being inconsiderate and stubborn, and that she was not to blame for it. Her heart was like a stone and her eyes felt heavy with unshed tears. She knew that her boredom and tiredness and her wish to go home were not as important to Jim as his and Rosetta's wish to stay there, just looking at each other. And she also knew that

Jim actually got pleasure from her annoyance, knowing that she could do nothing about it.

After a few more rounds, Jim finally decided that he was drunk and could not take more. It was only then that he decided to leave the mess. When they got to their house, Jim did not want to talk to Pam. He had once more started wondering what he had ever found so attractive in Pam that he had to marry her. That evening he saw no beauty in his wife. All he was conscious of was the strong physical attraction of Rosetta. He was especially annoyed when he realised that Rosetta, who had talked to him all evening, was now in the arms of another man. He felt frustrated and angry, and threw his shoes across the room as he took them off.

Pam looked at her husband with horror. She knew of course, that he was drunk. Somehow that explained his actions to some extent, but she asked softly, 'Jim, why are you throwing your shoes like that? What's the matter?'

'Woman!' he yelled at her, 'don't start nagging me! I brought you home and that's what you wanted. Go to sleep and leave me alone! And, one more thing, just one more thing woman: don't you ever dare harass me in front of my fellow officers again. Do you understand? Don't you ever dare again, or else!'

'But... but Jim, I didn't harass you! All I... ' Pam stammered. 'Will you shut up and go to sleep! I thought you were tired and sleepy when we were in the mess. So why don't you just sleep? Enough is enough, and if I hear one more word from you, you will regret it, I promise you!' Mutisya shouted at her.

Horrified, scared and confused, Pam got into bed without uttering another word. It was more than she could bear. It had been a horrifying revelation for her, for she knew at that moment, despite any doubts she'd had that the devil in Jim was aroused by that Rosetta girl. Even worse was the realisation that Jim wanted to be with Rosetta and not her, Pam, his wife. And this time, her whole world of illusion collapsed and disappeared into thin air, where it was beyond reach.

CHAPTER

9

♦ ♦ ♦ ♦

It was George's twentieth anniversary since joining the Nigerian Army, and he was giving a party to his fellow officers that evening to celebrate the occasion. George, himself, had had a wretched week and was not in a party mood. For the last two weeks since he'd met Pam, he had lived in a state of delirium. Almost every night, he was tormented with thoughts of his long-lost love, Janet. He constantly compared her with Pam; the similarity was almost enough to make him believe in reincarnation. For Pam was, in all respects, a carbon copy of his beloved Janet. What pained him most was his knowledge of how unhappy Pam was.

Mutisya was giving her a really bad time; George was sure of that. Why, only that morning, he recalled that Mutisya had told him that Pam was busy that evening and would be unable to attend his anniversary party. Of course, he knew Mutisya was telling him a lie, but being the gentleman he was, he had not pursued the issue further. There was actually no activity in the camp to account for Pam's 'prior engagement'.

So, as he sat quietly with his drink in the mess, contemplating the evening ahead, his suspicions were confirmed as he saw

Pam come in. George only needed one look at her to see the misery written on her face. The girl was a bundle of nerves. She looked tired and worn out. He had a feeling things were pretty bad for this poor girl, who looked so like Janet. Although Pam was little more than a total stranger to him, a woman married to a fellow officer and someone in whom he should not have any particular interest, he could not help but get worried and concerned. But, much as he tried not to think of Pam in a special way, he found it impossible. He remembered very well the first day she and Mutisya were supposed to be reunited. With that memory George knew, beyond any doubt, that Pam was in need of help.

'How are you, George?' she greeted him.

He stood up and stretched out his hand to greet her warmly. He was wearing his military uniform, which Pam had not seen before; she thought how well it suited him and made him look very handsome.

'You look very smart in your uniform,' she continued. 'Ah, of course! It is your military service anniversary party tonight. I almost forgot to congratulate you!' Then she immediately remembered that she and Mutisya had been invited to the party, but Mutisya had totally forbidden her to accept it.

'Join me for a drink Pam,' he said as he pulled up a chair for her. 'Jim not yet home?'

'Not yet,' she answered, without looking at him. George beckoned a waiter and ordered a drink for Pam. 'Is he in the field?' he enquired casually.

'Yes, he is. He's been out since yesterday, and hasn't shown up yet. Anyway, he has to be back tonight because we have visitors coming for supper. In fact, I have come here to get the drinks.'

'Oh, I see,' said George. The waiter brought the drinks. Sipping his, George said, 'I'm sorry you won't be able to come to my party. That's bad luck, you having guests for dinner the same evening I'm holding my party.'

'Yes, I'm sorry too. I really would have loved to come,' said Pam. There was silence, an awkward silence as both of them sank in their private thoughts about the other. In George, she saw consideration, love and kindness; the complete opposite of her husband, who was thoughtless and unpredictable.

Pam had been in Rhodesia now for two and a half months. Nearly two and a half months of total misery and heartbreak with Jim—quarrels about the slightest mistakes she made interspersed by occasional glimmers of hope, hints of his love, then suddenly thrown back into a state of loneliness, and hopelessness. Gradually, she had been forced to admit that their marriage was very nearly on the rocks, unless some miracle happened to save it and Jim, her husband, apparently mercilessly steering them both towards those rocks, without the slightest feelings for her.

Nowadays, she never could tell what mood he would be in when he came home. But one thing she was sure of was that he never appreciated anything she did or said. It was all 'bullshit' and 'rubbish' these days. There was no longer that husband/wife bond between them. Sometimes he would come home and demand attention from her but, much as she would pretend to respond, she couldn't totally. It was all so distasteful; she hated pretending to be the nice Pam she once was. She knew she had long lost any warm feelings towards him, and that such moments meant nothing to him anyway – he just wanted to satisfy his ego. He would always go back to his mistress, where he would thaw in her arms.

Although Mutisya would kiss her occasionally, she detested it. What would always follow was a long period of total negligence or some unfounded allegations that she had been unfaithful to him while he was 'away on duty' or that she was cold and stubborn. He had a whole repertoire of accusations, all of which he knew in his heart were unfounded and untrue. And there was always the shadow of his mistress, Rosetta, between them. She never dared mention her name, for fear of what would happen. Despite the dreadful atmosphere between them, Pam always had to put on a brave face which betrayed nothing of her misery. She even forced herself to write interesting letters both to her mother and Jim's family. He no longer wrote letters home. Days and nights seemed longer. She dreaded to see the sun set and darkness fall, for night spelt empty loneliness and misery for her. She was trying hard to get used to being alone all the time, but she longed for love and understanding – for the genuineness of a man's love which she had been denied for so long.

Now, as she sat there talking to George, she knew deep down in her heart that he was the man in whom she could find all that Jim lacked. George was a real gentleman, and that was the reason why Jim never liked him. Whenever George suggested an outing for the three of them, Jim refused the offer outright and later, when they got home, he would accuse her of being infatuated with the Nigerian Brigadier and even of conducting a love affair with him behind his back.

As the two talked and laughed in the mess that evening, Pam gradually relaxed and showed signs of real happiness. This pleased George more than anything else – to see Pam's face lit up with a smile was all that mattered to him then. But fate, as usual, played a trick on them for just as Pam had almost fully relaxed and was beginning to really feel happy, who should enter but her husband, Mutisya! His appearance sent a cold chill through her spine; her gay laughter and sense of fun vanished.

'Why, oh why should he come, just when I was beginning to enjoy myself?' Pam lamented within herself. George wasn't happy either at the appearance of Mutisya, but he tried not to show it... after all he George, was the intruder!

'Oh, good afternoon, Sir,' Mutisya greeted Brigadier Okonkwo.

'Good afternoon, Jim. Is it still afternoon or evening, I wonder?' Brigadier Okonkwo said, with a forced smile on his lips as he looked pointedly at his watch.

'Come and join us for a drink. You look tired and thirsty. A cool drink's just what you need!' he tried to sound casual.

Mutisya pulled up a chair from a nearby table and sat next to Pam. Brigadier Okonkwo beckoned a waiter and ordered drinks for them all. Mutisya was certainly thirsty, and no sooner had the waiter put the drinks on the table than he reached for his and downed it in a few gulps.

'So, how is it out there, Jim?' enquired Brigadier Okonkwo.

'Oh, not so bad, Sir. All is in order. I covered all the areas and it's quite quiet,' Mutisya answered.

'That's very encouraging,' put in Pam, who had been quiet all this time.

Kanini looked at her watch; six o'clock was round the corner. She must go home and prepare dinner. Major Mike and Rosetta were their guests for dinner that night. Jim had invited them without even consulting her. However, despite everything she was not going to show Jim that she was annoyed about it, so she did not want to be late with her cooking.

'Well, I'm sorry but I think I will have to leave you gentlemen,' Kanini excused herself, as she finished off her drink and got up.

'It's still early! Have another drink, Pam,' Brigadier urged her to stay.

'Oh, no. Thanks very much, but I really have to go and prepare supper. Thanks again, Brigadier all the same. Jim,' she turned to her husband as she stood up to go, 'can you bring the drinks. I have ordered them and ...'

'Sorry, Pam,' Jim interrupted her. 'I forgot to tell you, I don't think Mike and Rosetta can come to dinner after all. I was with Mike today and he said that Rosetta had a very bad cold and they wouldn't be coming tonight. So just sit down and have another drink. We will have supper here.'

'Oh dear, I'm sorry for her. When did she catch the cold? Ah well, she will be all right, I'm sure,' Pam said as she sat down again, hoping her words of concern had hidden the bitterness and suspicion she felt inside. Kanini knew that her husband's affair with Rosetta was an open secret, but she had never actually caught him out as she would have liked. Pam could never prove her accusations for it was only suspicions and speculation, and Jim knew he was safe. Unless he was ever caught.

After a few more rounds, Pam suggested that they go home. She was feeling tired and wanted to go home and sleep. Mutisya, too, felt drunk and sleepy and did not raise any objections to Pam's request. As they left, Pam wished Brigadier Okonkwo goodnight, and said she hoped he would enjoy his party. Mutisya shot her a black look and said nothing.

Their married quarters were not far, and being a bright night with a full moon and millions of stars twinkling like small diamonds, they decided to walk. Pam was a romantic woman at heart; she noticed the brightness of the moonlight and the stars – it was a romantic night, meant for lovers. Too bad! Romantic as the night was, there was to be no romance for her, and it pained her to think that Jim, probably never even noticed how romantic the night was and if he did, it was to think about his lover, Rosetta, and not her, his wife!

Once inside the house, Kanini was subjected to a torrent of abuse from her husband. The accusations were fired at her like bullets. Why had she gone to the mess on the pretext that she was going to get drinks for the evening? Couldn't she have waited for him to come home and go for the drinks himself? After all, he was the one who should cater for drinks, not her. Or were the drinks used as a cover-up, the main idea being to meet her lover, George? Why couldn't they have chosen a more discrete place to go to than the mess, where everybody knew that she was his wife? They could have had the decency to look for a better and more suitable place to conduct their affair!

Finally, there was dead silence. Kanini dared not utter a word. 'I think,' Mutisya suddenly continued, 'everybody including my own wife, is playing tricks on me! Mike lies to me that Rosetta is sick and therefore they cannot come for dinner, then I come home and what do I find? My wife flirting with a fellow officer!'

Pam stood still as she listened to Mutisya hurling a torrent of abusive words at her. Resentment welled up in her; she was completely fed up with these child-like outbursts of temper, without any reason whatsoever. This particular time, she was sure that his temper was generated from the fact that his friend, Mike, and his lover, Rosetta, were not coming for dinner. Not that he probably cared about Mike or the dinner, but for Rosetta's company – yes, Rosetta was the centre of attraction. Kanini finally let fly her temper too.

'Jim, it's all very well for you to lose your temper and call me names and accuse me of being unfaithful, but we both know that you're really angry because Mike let you down, thereby denying you the chance of being with Rosetta! You have no right... '

'Shut up, woman! Don't you dare! Don't you dare, or I'll... '

'Or you'll do what? Strangle me to death?' she mocked him.

'I'm ordering you to shut up, woman!' He made a move towards her.

'Don't stop me! I haven't quite finished yet! Jim, I might be your wife, but I don't think you have any right to behave the way you have. You have been away since yesterday and I have been lonely, alone with nobody to talk to, and when you come back instead of behaving like a loving husband, you come back to abuse me so shamelessly just because you cannot get things your own way! You know very well that I met George in the mess by sheer coincidence, and there was nothing sinister behind our meeting or sharing the table. It was pure coincidence, and you know it! You know it very well, Jim! You have the nerve to say unspeakable things about George, implicating him when you jolly well know he is innocent – and it's all to cover up your guilt about your affair! You refuse to invite him here for a drink to repay his kindness, and whenever he himself suggests that we get together you refuse, without giving him any good reason. You are jealous of him... you are jealous!'

There was a momentary silence, then Mutisya burst out sarcastically, 'Jealous! Huh! Jealous of what? Of a man who is old enough to be your father? You must be joking! Is that why you want me to develop my friendship with him, so that he can see you as often as he likes, without anybody raising a suspicious eyebrow because you are his "friend's" wife? Do you think I am a fool – a blind fool who can't see or think? You think I don't know what is going on between you and him? And you, my wife, are encouraging him. You may think I am a fool, my dear wife, but I can assure you I am not stupid!'

'OK, OK... you are entitled to your suspicious opinions, but even if that was the case – which it isn't, ' Pam retorted angrily, 'I could also point out to you that all along I've been aware of your affair with that Rosetta girl. I know your only reason to ask Mike for dinner was because you wanted to be with her and humiliate me in front of her. Oh, my God! How much longer will you go on pretending that you are Mike's friend, while you know very well it is not his company you want but that of his fiancée? Have you no shame? How can you not only cheat on your wife, but also cheat on your friend? The truth is that you have no feelings of friendship for Mike – you're just using him as a convenient cover-up for your little liaison with Rosetta!' she finished breathlessly.

'Wait a minute, woman…'

'No, I haven't finished yet!' she snapped back at him.

'All right, but before you start implicating people in your stupid allegations, you must get this straight – don't make the mistake of mentioning Rosetta's name!'

'I see; implicating Rosetta pains you because you know the truth and that truth is hurting you – very clever of you! I am the one who is blind and cannot see your reaction when you see Rosetta! I am not supposed to see or notice! Well, well, that is ironic. You want to implicate some innocent soul whom you know is not having an affair, and yet you want to deny that you are involved in an affair with Rosetta. That, to you, is an implication and not the truth – how clever. Let me tell you one thing Jim: I'm starved of love, and the, day I find somebody who loves me, I will not have any reservations! I will be jelly in his arms, just as you have been jelly in Rosetta's arms. Don't get me wrong, I am not suggesting that I am looking for somebody just to get even with you, no. I'm simply saying that if one day a man comes my way and loves me, I will certainly give in.'

'You have already given in – to your George – so what are you trying to tell me?'

'Soon, maybe soon, I will but make no mistake – you, my husband will be fully responsible for whatever happens. You will have driven me into ...'

'Into George's arms?' Mutisya finished for her. No answer came from Pam. She was quiet. That revelation had shocked Mutisya. He didn't know whether to slap her or abuse her further.

'All right then. If that is what my clever wife has discovered, then may I suggest that you go your way and I go mine! Whether I like Mike as a person or because of his fiancée is none of your business. I will do what I want, and likewise you can meet your lover, George, whenever you want.'

Pam suddenly grew wild with renewed anger. 'So, everything is once again designed to suit your plans. Well, I'm not going to allow you to implicate George in this. And Jim,' she spoke his name with a mocking tone, 'I will also not allow you to take advantage of Mike's gullibility while you carry on an affair with his fiancée behind his back. That you can be sure of! As she finished speaking, she walked into the kitchen to get herself a drink. She left a startled and speechless Mutisya staring after her in total disbelief at the knowledge that Pam knew the truth about his affair, but he was more disturbed about his apparent inability to handle his wife, who had shown herself in a new light to him that evening. He was completely cornered now. He was stripped of his pride. This was not like his Pam; his softly spoken Pam had been transformed into a brave, independent woman who had dared to answer her husband back and, what's more, confront him point blank with his love affair with Rosetta. He couldn't believe it.

In the kitchen, Kanini started to prepare supper. She herself had no appetite but she thought Jim might be hungry. The fact that they had quarrelled did not mean that she was not going to cook supper for him. After she had left Jim staring after her, he had composed himself and organised his thoughts. He, like all men, did not want to admit to his wife that he was sorry and regretted his behaviour. But, somehow, he had to try and contain the situation. They were in a foreign country and he did not want any scandalous gossip to embarrass him. He made up his mind to go in the kitchen and try to talk some sense into his wife. To talk or to confess – it didn't matter which word one used, but he must talk to her; he must react immediately before things got out of hand.

He went straight into the kitchen where he found Kanini busy making *ugali* while some meat stew was cooking on the other hotplate. 'Pam, I know you have summed me up as a bad husband who is moody and cannot keep his promises. Well, you are entitled to form your own opinion, but one thing I want to make clear to you is that I love you, Pam. Think and say what you will, but that is the truth. I love you honey.'

There was silence, save for the noise coming from the boiling and shimmering of the cooking stew and *ugali*. Kanini, feeling provoked, looked at him with cold, stony eyes which made Mutisya feel genuinely both ashamed and embarrassed.

'I know very well you hate me, Jim,' she told him flatly. 'I don't care so much about your love – not anymore, and certainly not after tonight's disclosure, I... '

'Pam, don't be such a baby! You know damned well that I don't hate you! It's just that, just that... Oh hell!'

'Just what? Just that you don't know who to choose? You cannot make up your mind between Rosetta and I? I'll help you make up your mind! I'll.'

'Pam, listen to me baby,' Mutisya tried to be as calm as possible, 'It's not like that, Pam baby. Oh, how can I explain this to you? It's just one of those things temporary things that happen to a guy when he is away from his wife. I mean, it isn't anything much between Rosetta and I. It's only...'

'Oh, I see! It's only one of those things that happen to a guy when he is away from his wife. What about a wife when she is away from her husband? Are the same things supposed to happen to her? Well, are they Jim? Answer me. Anyway, I have already told you what I feel. You don't have to lecture me on how a man behaves when he is away from his wife. I know it! I already know it, from experience, and that is quite enough.'

'So I see. But let me tell you one thing if you are going to start another scene, then you are looking for trouble, my dear silly wife,' he said, sarcastically.

'And did you, my dear husband,' she said, matching his sarcasm, 'come here in the kitchen to create a scene? Well, if that was your intention then I'm not going to be part of it, but I must make one thing clear to you also – one more thing.'

'And what's this command that I'm supposed to take from my dear wife, if I may ask?'

'You can be as sarcastic as you like, it doesn't bother me anymore. But I am not going to have you kick me around left, right and centre every time you come home, when I know very well that you no longer love me and you haven't got the slightest feelings for me. It's all pretence!'

'Wait a minute!' Jim moved towards her and grabbed her shoulder. 'Who says that I don't love you? The mere fact that a guy dates another woman does not mean that he doesn't love his wife. At least, it does not apply to me and you know it!'

'Oh, is that so?' the words came from her mouth as a faint whisper.

'Yes, it is so Pam. I love you. I have loved you all the time. Please love me, Pam... love me, just a little...' He took her in his arms and kissed her first on the cheek and then full on her mouth. She was not moved a bit by his wild kiss. Neither was she placated by his words. She pushed him away. His kiss had roused the devil in her. She hated him! Hated him for feigning love for her, for pretending that he had feelings for her. He was kissing her, yet he did not mean it – and she knew it. She stood still. Her heart seemed to have stopped beating. With bitterness she looked at her one-time lover; she had once loved him, loved him so much that she thought she would die if she did not marry him. He had seemed to be the most handsome man she had ever seen, so romantic and loving, with beautiful pleading eyes – just what a girl would see in a man she is in love with. But now... now... where, oh, where had all those qualities gone?' As she stood there looking at him, she only saw an ugly figure, someone who had hurt her so badly. She hated him with all her heart.

'Let's not pretend anymore, Jim, that there is any feeling between us. There's no question of you being in love with me. You know it just as much as I do. For that matter, everybody knows that you are in love with somebody else's fiancée, and you are a married man too. I'm not prepared to go on like this any longer, you pretending to love me while you actually hate me for coming between you and your lover. All you live for are your meetings with that girl. I haven't the stamina left in me anymore.'

Before she could say anything else, Mutisya walked out of the kitchen, banging the door behind him. He went straight to bed. When the supper was ready, she put it in two serving dishes and carried it to the sitting-room, thinking that he was still there. The full glass of untouched whisky and water made Kanini think that Mutisya was probably in the toilet. She placed the food on the table and set a place for Jim. She went back to the kitchen, and after ascertaining that she had switched everything off, she proceeded to the bedroom.

To her annoyance, she found him lying on the bed, fully awake. 'Your supper is on the table,' she told him, forcing the words to come out.

'I don't want it! I don't feel like eating!' he snapped at her. Pam said nothing. She started to undress herself, not at all sure whether she wanted to share the bed with him that night.

'Pam!' He almost whispered her name, in a completely different tone from the one he had used a few minutes earlier. 'Come to me, Pam,' he reached out and pulled her down onto the bed.

'Jim!' she snapped at him. 'If you have a shred of decency left in your heartless heart, you'll leave me alone!'

'Listen, Pam... ' he started.

'I will not listen to you, Jim. I have listened to you all evening and I think it's enough. Don't think that I'm such a fool, or maybe a toy for you to play with when you feel like it. Jim,' she was now breathless, 'what you need is a robot for a wife – some kind of machine you can switch on and off when you feel like it, a machine that you will not need to love.'

'OK, OK. Just before you say something you might regret, let's settle this unfortunate incident. Let's discuss our problem like a husband and wife, shall we?'

'Settle what "unfortunate incident" by discussing with you as my husband?' she retorted sarcastically.

'I think you're getting rather hysterical, Pam. You've brooded over this whole thing for too long, honey. Just cool down and let me explain. I think it is so ridiculous! We just can't go on like this. I've told you that I love you... and I'm being very honest, I swear it...I do!'

CHAPTER
10

♦ ♦ ♦ ♦

Pam was not in the least moved by this second appeal from Jim at first. She shook her head as she tried to get away from him. But it was all quite disturbing. She did not know whether to believe his appealing words or not; she had heard the same words over and over again and she had forgiven him, but still he carried on just where he'd left off. It just didn't make sense to Pam. It was all so pointless. She shot him a look that implied he was still telling her lies. To her, Jim had assumed this behaviour as his lifestyle – lying to her every day. She was so uncertain of what he said to her; he never kept his promises and his moods were as unpredictable, choosing one minute to be sweet and charming, and hurling abuse at her the next. However, one thing she knew for sure was that his caressing hands held no passion or meaning for her; they just made her hate him even more.

Mutisya never accepted defeat, and was absolutely set on getting back into his wife's good books. He was, tonight of all nights, determined to make peace with Pam, and would not give up even after her wild protests to let her go, to leave her alone.

'All right. I admit I have taken Rosetta out, but that was before you came here, Pam. Mike and I are friends, as you know, and he occasionally asked me to keep Rosetta busy while he was away on long recess. Pam darling, try to understand. If anybody is wagging their tongues about Rosetta and me, it's only idle gossip. Some people smear other people's names with unfounded allegations; and, of course, in a place like this where most people are idle all day long, with nothing much to occupy their minds, what do you expect? Somebody only has to be seen talking to a girl once or twice or sitting with her, and they soon blow it all up out of proportion, and start gossiping that the two of them are lovers. It's all just jealous talk!'

All the time that Mutisya was talking, Pam was, for some reason unknown to her, imagining George and in her mind comparing the two. Suddenly, it seemed to her that Jim was the ugliest creature that she had ever seen, made worse by his pathetic pleading for forgiveness, which was clearly all pretence. He no longer excited her in any way at all. Looking at his mouth, she genuinely wondered how or why she had ever allowed him to kiss her, and how she ever yielded to him. On the other hand, she imagined George to be the most good-looking man she had ever met in her life. More importantly, he was kind and so loving. This feeling made her shiver suddenly. She realised that she was no longer in love with her husband, Jim. Her once adored husband had killed all the love she had for him – every grain of it. Slowly, mercilessly and without care he had murdered all that was in her for him, and that night, of all nights, she was like a block of ice in his arms, hard and very, very cold.

Mutisya continued to plead with her and it surprised her to think that he could have the impudence to lie to her so many times about Rosetta. Because of her good heart she always believed and forgave him. He had sworn many times to be good to her, abandon his previous ways and be faithful and loving. She did not know what to say or do. Part of her wanted to forgive him, yet another part did not want to. The one thing that disturbed her was the knowledge that she didn't love him anymore. She never could love him again as she once had – that had become history! She could never respect him or have confidence in him again and, worse still, even now as he pleaded with her to forgive him, she could not believe his emotional outbursts, could not trust him, ever! That hurt very much. It was very unfortunate that the night he chose to play the part of a passionate lover to his wife, was the night she felt she hated him, despised him and detested his kisses more than she'd ever thought possible. She had never loved anybody the least as she did Jim that particular night.

It was in the early hours of the morning, when, tired and confused, she eventually softened a little and talked to him, but it was only because she still felt that it was her duty as a wife to try all she could to stop their marriage from falling apart – more so in a foreign country. She knew, in her heart, that as soon as she gave in it would not be long before Jim went back to his old ways, yet she felt compelled to try, at least for the time they were in a foreign land.

One evening Pam learned with great happiness that Major Mike had been recalled to his original unit to be assigned other duties. She imagined that this meant the end of Jim's affair with Rosetta, since he would take her with him. The period that followed the departure of Mike and Rosetta spelt more misery and harassment for Pam than she had expected. Mutisya was very moody. His atrocious behaviour was like a tiger with a sore foot. He abused her for every slight mistake she made. In her heart, she knew why he was behaving like that; Rosetta's sudden departure had meant the end of the affair and this had made him wild with rage. However, even with this knowledge, she said nothing about it.

Kanini's hopes of eventual calm after the storm were short lived. If Pam, or anyone else, had thought that with Rosetta's exit Jim would become the devoted husband, they would be very mistaken. For soon after, there was another woman in his life. Marie, a childless woman nearly twice the age of Pam was his next mistress. Soon the rumour of Mutisya's affair with the older woman spread like fire in a dry jungle. It was the talk of the camp, and soon things started getting out of hand. Pam finally had to talk to her husband, despite her reluctance and her negative feelings towards him.

'Jim,' she told him one evening while they were having supper, 'it's all up to you now. I have been completely unable to control you where women are concerned, and I have given up ever trying again, but you are letting yourself down and this, I feel, is not very good for your career.'

'Pam, honey,' he said, soothingly, 'what is it now? Why do you listen to what people say? I thought you would have understood by now how malicious some people can be – spreading unfounded gossip against others just to spoil their reputations and hurt their feelings. Pam, forget what other people say and you will find that eventually they will get tired of talking and will keep quiet. And by the way,' he said after a moment, changing the topic, 'I want to take you out for a drink after we finish eating, so just finish your food and get dressed up – it's a chilly evening.'

And so Pam, not wishing to argue, went to the bedroom after her supper and got dressed up. They went out, but no matter how hard he pretended to be loving, Pam knew that he was in love, not with her, his wife, but with another woman. From his artificial and forced behaviour, Pam could tell that she was a real bore to him these days. Things being the way they were, Pam herself made little effort to break the ice between them. She was completely fed up with his insincere apologies and had no illusions about how he really felt. In return, she felt that she no longer cared what happened to him.

Throughout all her secret torture and inner sufferings of both mind and body, only one person in her whole small world shared them with her, albeit unknown to her. Perhaps it would have made life easier for her if only she had known that someone thought of her as a very special person and shared all her misery. Brigadier Okonkwo was all aware from the beginning that things were very wrong in Mutisya's household. He knew that Pam, once healthy and full of vigour and life, was nowadays nothing more than a bundle of broken nerves. She had grown thin, looked tired and everything on her indicated that she had lost hope in life. This touched George to his heart, and although he knew it was not the right thing to do, he swore he would talk to her and maybe find out if there was anything he could do to help her escape from that miserable shell in which she was living.

Then one day, as fate would have it, Brigadier Okonkwo was driving for pleasure in some lonely woods, trying to figure out how he could best handle the delicate situation. It was a cool Sunday afternoon and so he did not expect to have any company in those lonely woods. However, he noticed in the distance a Land Rover discreetly parked under a shady tree. He took out his binoculars and looked. What he saw made his blood freeze in his very veins. He found himself shaking all over, not – with cold but with rage. It was the most shocking thing he had ever seen in his life but, as much as he regretted having looked, he could not help but feel a murderous rage against the man sitting on the bonnet of the Land Rover. For there was Jim, happily kissing and laughing with his mistress without shame or regard for his poor wife, whom he'd reduced to a total wreck both mentally and physically.

George could not stand it; he drove away in anger. He felt that if he stayed a second longer and watched Jim laughing so happily with that woman, he would have pulled out his gun and gladly shot him.

He drove straight to the camp, to Mutisya's house. Pam, poor Pam, was resting on a chair listening to soothing music coming from the stereo in the sitting-room while reading some magazines. By instinct, she went to look through the window as soon as she heard a car roaring to a stop in front of her house. She thought it was Jim, but to her great surprise and inward pleasure it was George. She did not wait for him to knock but went straight to open the door for him.

'Good afternoon, Pam,' he offered his hand as he greeted her.

'Good afternoon, George. And how are you?' she responded. 'Come in. You look worn out. Where have you been?'

'I do feel a bit tired but I didn't think I looked so. I have been out in the field... '

'Oh, I'm sorry, George!' she interrupted. 'Do sit down, please. Jim is not home but I hope he will be back soon. He went out on a recce early this morning, and he is not yet back.' She started making excuses for her husband automatically, not having the slightest idea that George knew exactly where Jim was and what he was doing.

'A recce, indeed... what a cad the guy is!' George reflected silently. 'Oh, I see. I was just passing by and I thought that I might perhaps pop in and say hello. I, em...,' he coughed deliberately while trying to find the right words, 'I... er... hope I did not interrupt your siesta, Pam, by coming without notice?'

'Oh, no, no, George, not at all! On the contrary, I er…,' she stopped. Pam didn't want to let anybody see her misery or to openly make it known that she was unhappy, despite the fact that it was common knowledge among most people that she was actually very unhappy with Jim. 'What can I offer you to drink?' she continued.

'Nothing at the moment. I have just had a drink in the mess,' he lied.

'No, no, you must have something! With this hot weather one needs to drink all the time. You can have something mild, at least,' she insisted.

'All right. I'll have some juice, please. Any juice you have will do,' he agreed at last.

Kanini poured the juice for both herself and George. They drank in silence, but George found it difficult to swallow the juice. There seemed to be something blocking his throat. He could guess the reason why... one look at Pam, sitting opposite him so innocently, quite unaware of what her husband was doing. He felt he could wring his neck! One more look at Pam and he felt the tears welling up in his eyes. She was such a pathetic sight. If at that moment fate had brought Mutisya home, he would have killed him. He couldn't bear it any longer; he couldn't sit back and watch Jim slowly destroy Pam.

'Pam!' he suddenly spoke her name emotionally. 'I don't want to hurt you anymore than you've been hurt already, but I do want you to talk to me in strict confidence about your life out here. Make no mistake, I'm not trying to probe into your personal life; neither do I wish to interfere in your marriage. Although,' he swallowed hard as he tried to force the words out of his mouth, 'I will if need be.'

Those last words said so emotionally by George, touched Pam so much that tears started flowing uncontrollably from her eyes. George nearly regretted his mission when he saw her crying, but he quickly pulled himself together. Most of all, he wanted to gather Pam in his arms and kiss her, kiss and comfort her, but again he painfully controlled the urge. He spoke to her again, softly.

'Hush, please Pam, don't cry. I don't want to see you cry. I only hope I did not say anything to hurt you Pam and if I have, please forgive me.'

'No, no George,' Pam sobbed the words out. 'You have not said anything to hurt me and there is nothing to be sorry for. George, I er... I... it's just that I cannot bear it, George. It is far too much for me. I cannot hold my tears back, much as I want to.'

'I understand, Pam. I really do understand. However, trust me and pour your heart out to me and don't be afraid.'

'George, you don't know how much I appreciate your concern over me. I do trust you, George, and I'm not afraid to tell you what my life has been like. In any case, most of the people around here know and talk about it openly. It's so humiliating, George.'

'Yes, I know,' George cleared his throat and reflected back to the first time that he met Pam; the day she arrived in Rhodesia from Kenya. A beautiful, lively young lady, totally in love with her husband, and full of life. Then he'd compared her to a beautiful young rose bud, early in the morning, fresh with the morning dew but now, all that beauty was gone and all that remained was a withering, dried-up flower. For the umpteenth time, George wondered why some men took the trouble to marry in church, to exchange those sacred marriage vows only to break them within no time at all and without a care or thought for the other party.

George, being a music lover like Kanini, recalled an old record in which the singer remembered his mother advising him to 'take time to know her,' since marriage was not an overnight affair. Presumably, the young man had wanted to marry his girlfriend immediately but the mother, having more foresight, advised her son not to rush into marriage. 'Pam should have taken time to know Jim,' George reflected.

'George, I do thank you very much for your concern. I really appreciate it. I don't know how much you know about Jim, but I'm sure you have heard the latest gossip. George, I admit all is not well with me and Jim. Not anymore.' She paused for a while and then gathered more strength to continue. It hurt her so deeply that even after trying to be courageous enough to talk about it, she could only whisper.

'George, Jim has changed a lot since he started his current affair with that divorced woman, Marie. What is worse is that he makes it so obvious, and yet he denies everything. I sometimes wish he would stay away and never come home at all, because when he does come it's nagging, nagging and quarrelling all the time. He never leaves me alone. Sometimes, I'm not quite sure if it is my fault. I blame myself for his affairs! Perhaps I don't give him as much attention as he feels he should get from me, or love for that matter, or maybe... '

'My dear Pam,' he cut her short; he couldn't bear to hear her blaming herself for being responsible for her husband's behaviour, 'there is always a limit for everything. I mean, even a rubber band can only stretch so far, and when you try to stretch it further, it will of course break without warning. So even a human being, and this includes women too for that matter, can only tolerate and be patient for a limited time. Thereafter, you cannot take in anymore; you become saturated with problems and frustrations and any further pressure will spell disaster.'

There was silence. Pam quietly thought over the whole situation and felt so moved that she could not hold back the tears any longer. To see her weeping made George feel very uneasy. He would have given anything on earth to hold her in his arms and comfort her, but the best he could do was to offer her his silk handkerchief to wipe away her tears.

'Pam,' he said gently to her, 'don't let life defeat you. You are a very courageous girl, and I'm sure you will be all right.' Easier said than done! He knew it would not be as easy as it sounded for Pam to take in more of her husband's lies and bullying. He was a playboy. Yes, that's what he was, a perfect playboy. George felt defeated himself for not being able to change Jim or comfort Pam as he would have loved.

It was long after six in the evening and Jim had not yet come back home. 'I think I should be going, Pam,' he announced emotionally, and with such a heavy heart that he could cry. He alone was aware of what actually kept her husband so late. 'I hope Jim will not be out much longer – he should be coming home soon, I think,' he added absent-mindedly.

'Yes, I think he should be back any time now. As a matter of fact, he had promised to be back by four o'clock. I think he must be held up somewhere,' Pam added quite innocently.

'Held up somewhere indeed!' George nearly screamed the words out but just managed to stop them from escaping his mouth in time. There was silence as Pam thought about how kind and handsome George looked.

'You are one in many men, George. You are the kindest, tenderest and the most handsome man, in heart and physically I've ever met. You are always smiling, that genuine smile that assures a broken heart of hidden happiness – you smile that smile without any pretence. You

have all the good qualities that a woman needs in a man. And poor Janet, she missed all that goodness. She will never know, God rest her soul in peace; and as for me, God have mercy. I didn't know the kind of a man I was tying that holy knot with. I was blinded by what I then thought was love. I couldn't see, I couldn't! Oh God, I wish, oh how I wish I waited! Waited for somebody like you, George, to come my way. I'm sure even back home I could have found myself a kinder person to marry. If only I had waited. Too late I realise I cannot retrace my footsteps. I cannot gather up the milk that is already spilt. I'm done for and even if I wanted to untie that knot with Jim, I couldn't! Even though you, George, care for me it is much too late. I belong lawfully to Jim! But, my soul, my whole heart and body belongs to no one, that's the tragedy. I have nobody to live for, save for my mother. ' Kanini's thoughts were racing as she sat there opposite George.

George too was silently wrapped up in his own thoughts. He had realised without any doubt that he loved Pam... loved her and wanted her for himself more than anything else on earth. This revelation did not really shock him. He had known it deep down all along. From the day he had set eyes on her. It was a sweet-bitter love for him since she belonged to somebody else, a fellow officer, from a foreign country and, what more, it seemed to him that she was still in love with her soldier husband. *'Ah, well,'* he thought, *'once we part, after the peace-keeping forces are withdrawn from Rhodesia, which should be soon, I will never set eyes on her again. She will go back to Kenya, her country, and disappear from my life. She will be lost to me forever, just like Janet!'* This last thought made him feel wild. He lost his head momentarily and could only think of her. 'Pam,' he spoke to her in a whisper, 'I know it's all very wrong... you being a colleague's wife... but... but... oh, I mustn't see you again. I really mustn't.'

'Why, George?' she asked him, with a confused trembling voice. 'What makes you say that? What have I done to you? I thought we were... I thought we were good friends, George. I don't understand why you...'

'Pam,' he stopped. He stood up and walked to the window. Pam followed him with her misty eyes, blinded by unshed tears. When he turned and faced her, he was wild with the desire to hold her in his arms and kiss her – kiss her as she had never been kissed before. 'Pam, I don't know how you feel about me, but the honest truth is that I love you, I love you Pam! Don't you see... don't you understand? I have loved you all along and because I cannot be with you, cannot express my love for you the way I feel I should, I must stop seeing you! That's why, Pam. I cannot deny my love any longer than I already have.'

Hearing those words of confession of his love for her, Pam's small world seemed to spin. She felt on top of the world! George himself was telling her that he loved her! Confessing his love for her right there, in that very room, standing right there opposite her! It all sounded like a beautiful dream, yet it was no dream. It was very real, so real that she willingly shed tears of both joy and sadness.

She became tongue-tied when she tried to speak. Then suddenly, she felt some strength in her and ran straight into George's arms. 'Oh, George, I love you too! I think I have loved you ever since that afternoon you took me for that long ride. George, please don't stop coming to see me! I can't bear it!' In no time, the two were enveloped in each other's arms, the man comforting and whispering loving words to the weeping woman.

'Pam,' he finally said, gathering what strength was left in him, for he felt so weak that he could faint, 'honey, it is all so ironic – us two loving each other, since we cannot belong to each other. I wouldn't mind if I was recalled back to Nigeria this very second, for I would take you with me and take care of you and love you always. You are adorable, Pam! You are everything that a man would go to jail for! Pam, I would kidnap you and take you to the end of the world and live with you there if need be!'

'Oh George, how I would love that…me looking after you and caring for you. Oh George, what are we going to do now? It will never work out like that. I'm tied to Jim in holy matrimony, until death do us part.'

'I know Pam. Don't let that worry you, though. That is no reason why I cannot love you. With or without that ceremony, you know you are still lovable, my darling Pam. The problem is what is going to happen to us, now that we know we love each other!' There was a moment of silence then George said, 'Those who were before us were right when they said, "Love is like measles, all the worst when it comes late in life!" Pam, that is how my love for you is.'

'Oh George, and how right they were! I feel I could die for your sake, George, if that's what it would cost me for loving you!'

'Pam, honey, what makes it worse is that I know you and Jim no longer love each other. Your marriage is on the rocks and I know you live like total strangers. I know you are trying very hard to save your marriage from breaking up Pam, but you are fighting a losing battle. A losing battle because it is one-sided. It's only you who has the will to make the marriage survive. I'm afraid your husband is working hard to do the exact opposite – to see that the marriage breaks up. Pam, I don't know whether I will be able to sit back and watch you go through this torture and humiliation much longer.'

'Perhaps I'd better ask Jim to send me back home, to Kenya, where I'll find love and care in my mother's house?' Pam said, as she clung to George's hand as if all her life depended on it or on what he would say to her.

'No, Pam, you cannot do that. I will not allow you to do it! You cannot go! Give me time to think of a solution, will you Pam? Of course, I know it's not going to be easy, but let's just give it plenty of thought and then wait and see what happens.'

Pam was so touched by what George was telling her, that she wept on his shoulder openly. With his arms around her, she felt so secure that she would have given her whole life to belong to him. For the first time, she confessed her regrets at ever having married Jim. If only she could retrace her footsteps, if only a miracle would have happened so that she had met George and married him instead.

George looked at his watch. He must be going – time was running out and he did not dare wait any longer in case Jim turned up. He could not face him – not because he felt guilty for expressing his love for his wife, but because he felt he could murder Jim for all the wrongs he had done to Pam. He held her tightly against his chest momentarily and then kissed her passionately.

'I'll have to go, Pam, but I will see you soon, very soon. Meanwhile, take care of yourself. Promise me you will, Pam?' The last few words were said in an emotional whisper.

'I promise you, George, I will take care of myself,' Pam's tone was equally passionate.

After George left her, she felt so weak and desperate that she had to hold onto the arm of the chair for support. She could not understand why, but she suddenly felt a warm wave of well-being sweep all over her body. She felt faint in the body but her spirit was strong because of what George had told her. Pam did not know for how long she sat there, reliving the memories of George, until she finally fell asleep.

Pam did not hear Jim come in, for she was in a deep contented sleep. Jim, being in very high spirits and drunk with happiness after having spent the day with Marie, did not want to wake her up in case she asked him questions and spoilt his happiness. He walked slowly past her and went into the bedroom. He was feeling cold and decided that a warm shower would warm and relax him. It was while he was taking his shower that Pam woke up and heard him. She had a splitting headache. She went to the bedroom and fetched some painkillers which she took.

Pam was not one to ask questions and Jim was certainly not one to give explanations. Luckily for Pam, she had some wonderful memories to cherish, and she felt happier when Jim went out and left her alone. She needed to be alone and free to think about George. She was now sure that what she felt for him was real love; she missed him, missed him so much that she thought she would go crazy! For two consecutive days, she had a non-stop headache and a loss of appetite. Jim, of course, did not notice anything but was trying hard to act the perfect husband, by taking Pam out for drinks and not picking arguments with her. She knew this treatment would last as long as she did not complain about anything. However, luck was not on her side, for after a few weeks of relative tranquility on the home front, she fell ill. She had been doing some general cleaning in the house when she experienced a searing pain, and then suddenly felt dizzy and fell. Fortunately, she managed to crawl to the telephone extension and dialled the officers' mess. Soon the ambulance was at her house and she was taken to the dispensary where she was admitted. The doctor attending her diagnosed acute appendicitis and said an immediate operation was necessary.

For a full week, Pam lay in the hospital. When she had recovered sufficiently Jim took her home with the doctor's instructions to make sure that she had complete bed-rest, without which she would take a long time to heal.

'She is very weak,' the doctor added. The doctor's instructions, of course, meant that Jim would have to come home early to do the cooking, some washing and ironing of his uniforms and even help to sponge-bath his wife. It was not a welcome task for Jim at all, especially since it meant less time with his mistress, Marie. It was this curtailing of his time with his mistress that annoyed Jim most, rather than the errands he now had to do. He grumbled and complained about Pam not appreciating what he was doing for her.

'For heaven's sake, Pam, pull yourself together! Don't look so pathetic – you've not been that ill...'

'But Jim, I appreciate everything you do, I...'

'You don't and you know it!' Jim retorted. Jim's anger and frustrations had been building up and he was waiting for an opportunity to present itself when Pam would make a small mistake so that he could release them. When he saw that such an opportunity was not going to be forthcoming, he had to create it himself.

'Pam,' he almost shouted her name. 'Tell me; just tell me how many men do you know who would have the patience to take orders from their invalid wives? Tell me!'

'Jim, I do not have the strength to argue with you. I... ' She could not go on; tears started rolling down her cheeks.

'Jim, Jim, Jim... ' he called his own name sarcastically. 'Ha! I know what you are doing. You are taking advantage of your so-called weakness so that you can order me around! You are such a pretender! I just can't find words to describe what a pretender you are! And by the way, you know I don't believe in tears so don't bother with your crocodile tears... weeping, weeping, weeping... a waste of water!'

'All right, Jim; Pam said weakly. 'Enough is enough. You have your own opinion but please, if you have any human decency, leave me alone. Just leave me alone!' She sobbed the words with such bitterness in her heart, she wished she could die.

CHAPTER
11

♦ ♦ ♦ ♦

Jim was in a murderous mood the following day. To calm his nerves, he decided to pay a surprise visit to his mistress. She had just returned from town when he arrived.

'You don't look too happy, Jim. Are you sick or something?' she asked him, looking slightly uneasy.

'Oh, I guess I'm just tired, that's all.'

'Oh, I see. What can I get you to drink?' she asked as she entered the kitchen.

'Usual, darling.'

They both sat on the couch and had their drinks. Then Mutisya announced that he was going to lie on the bed for a short while and asked Marie to wake him up after an hour or so.

'No! No, Jim. You can't go to bed and leave me here alone,' she protested.

'Then come with me!'

'No, I don't want to sleep. I want to stay here and drink.'

'Then stay here and drink,' he told her as he stood up to go.

Marie caught his hand and tried to detain him.

'Why don't you want me to go into your bedroom, Marie?' he asked her as he freed his hand and walked to the bedroom. On opening the door, Jim froze. The bed was unmade and there, on top of it, lay a man's shirt and coat.

'I see. That explains it all,' he said, icily. 'Yeah! I see why you were against my coming in here!' Turning to face her squarely, he said, 'Marie, I want the truth.'

There was a long silence. At last he spoke again, 'Marie, I told you I want the truth. Do you hear?' He shook her by the shoulders so violently that it hurt her. She screamed a little.

'All right, you want to know the truth; you will know it. The shirt and the coat belong to a friend of mine,' she said, and then remained quiet.

'Go on! Go on, Marie. Your man friend, is it?' 'Yes, my man friend.'

'You wretched woman!' Mutisya lost his temper. 'You liar! You've lied to me all along. You've made a fool of me! I quarrelled with my wife because of you – and now this! When can women be trusted? When will they stop telling lies and tell the truth? I thought you were mature and sensible – but I regret the day we first met! Little wonder, then, that your husband died of a heart attack! Poor fellow! You are nothing more than a prostitute... you are... you ...!'

All the time Mutisya was hurling abuse at her, Marie became so worked up that when she finally spoke, Mutisya did not believe his ears were hearing right.

'Yes, you regret you quarrelled with your wife!' she emphasized the word 'wife'. 'Hmm... that most talked about wife of yours!' 'What about? Talked about what?' he asked impatiently.

'Oh nothing, nothing,' she said, sensing that he had taken the bait.

Jim lost his temper again. He grabbed her by the shoulders once more and then threw her on the unmade bed. 'I demand to know what is said about my wife!'

'Don't pretend you don't know! At least I'm better off. Even if I go around with a million men, I'm nobody's wife – If I was, at least I would keep it a secret.'

'Wait a minute! What are you trying to say? Are you suggesting that it's being said that my wife is being unfaithful?' he asked, incredulously.

'Hmm, precisely. That's just what I'm trying to tell you,' she smiled, wickedly.

'You are crazy! You are a mad woman! What lies are you talking...?'

'Lies or no lies, you jolly well know it is the truth!' she was triumphant now.

Mutisya waited to hear no more. He walked out, got into his Land Rover and drove away. On his way home, he tried to weigh things up. *'Pam...unfaithful to me? No, no, that is out of the question!'* He knew his Pam. She was not the type to ... *'No! No! It just can't be. George is a decent chap. Not the kind of man who would behave that way. It's not possible. Just not possible. But then, if everybody knows and is talking about it...'*

His thoughts were still in turmoil when he got home. Pam, the dutiful wife, served her husband with tea, after which he asked for a whisky and water. Supper time soon came. Pam laid the table but Mutisya refused to eat. 'Aren't you feeling hungry? You must have had a heavy lunch!' Pam joked.

'Yes, indeed – heavy lunch,' he said, sarcastically.

Pam sensed there was something wrong.

'What is the matter, Jim? You don't look too happy.'

'You dare ask me such a question!' he snapped back. 'I am sorry! I was just asking...'

'Yes, just asking!' He was being sarcastic again and she knew it.

'As if you needed to ask!'

'Oh, by the way, Jim;' she said, trying to change the subject, 'I am thinking of going home. I think it would be better. What do you think?' As no reply came from Jim she continued, 'Can you make the arrangements for my return to Kenya?'

'What has made you want to go back home? I thought you were... were enjoying your stay here.'

'Enjoying it or not enjoying it, Jim, I want to go home. I'm homesick.'

'Oh, I see. And is your Brigadier George accompanying you?'

Pam nearly fainted at the mention of George's name.

'Jim, you are crazy! You must be drunk. You...you…'

'I'm neither crazy nor drunk, my dear innocent wife.'

'Then just what do you mean by asking me if George is accompanying me to Kenya, when you know very well he is not even a Kenyan?'

'Don't answer a question with a question! I asked you a very simple and straightforward question, and all I want is a simple, straightforward answer from you. And if you want me to repeat it for you, I will...'

'All right. George is not accompanying me to Kenya. Are you satisfied?'

'Only to a point. Tell me, when did you last see George, Pam?' 'Another simple question, Jim, eh?'

'Yes, my dear Pamela. Another simple question,' he said sarcastically, deliberately calling her by her full first name.

'I see. Before I give you a simple answer, would you tell me just what you are trying to get at, James?' She too could be sarcastic. Her nerves were on edge now, her pulses racing in fear of another scene which she fully anticipated from the look of things. She braced herself for the tirade that was to follow.

'Answer my question, woman! I've already told you that you don't answer a question with another question. Tell me, when did you last see and talk to George?' Jim raised his voice.

'All right! I saw and talked to George today.' The expression on Jim's face at her reply warned her of greater danger.

'Then that confirms it.'

'Confirms what?' Her whole body was trembling and she felt hot with perspiration.

'Hmm ... you really are the limit! You even have the cheek to ask me such a question as if you don't know what I'm talking about!'

'Jim, I...I...I don't know what you are talking about.'

'I see. That's very, very funny indeed, beautiful and faithful wife. '

'It's not funny, Jim. It's... It's...'

'Calm down, my dear wife,' he said, even more sarcastically. 'You don't have to pretend. As they say, a thief has only forty days. On the fortieth day, he or she is caught. So you see, my dear faithful wife, your forty days are up!'

'Jim, will you please explain this nonsense to me? Just what is happening? Haven't I the right to know what you are accusing me of?'

'Well, well, since you obviously want to carry this charade of innocence through to the end, I will tell you. I'm very disgusted that everybody knows and is talking about your affair with George. I, of course...'

'Jim, what are you talking about? You know it's not true! What are you saying? You... you...,' Pam was aghast. She could not understand all these unfounded accusations against her and George. George who, since the day she had arrived in Rhodesia, had never said or done anything to suggest that he was in love with her until a week ago. It was only that day they had actually admitted to their love for each other and George had taken a low profile because of his respect for Jim. Pam regretted George's visit early that day. As a good-hearted man, he had only come to find out how Pam was recovering.

'Jim, you may say what you like, but it is not true, and you know it! There is absolutely nothing between George and I. It's all a story made up by whoever it is that wants to slander me. They just want to tarnish my name and give George a bad reputation. Oh, they are a horrible, filthy lot of scandalous rumour mongers! And you... you, my husband, listened to their unworthy gossip? Jim,' she spoke his name in an icy tone, 'are you forgetting your own scandal, you and Rosetta and now Marie? I dare say if someone has told you that I'm carrying on an affair with George behind your back – and you know it's not true – then I can assure you that whoever it is wants to spoil my name and smear George's. Perhaps you've even made up the whole story yourself just to cover yourself... '

'Hang on, woman! I got this information from a very reliable source, somebody who has no malice, somebody I fully trust, someone... ' his voice trailed off as he pictured Marie's face as she'd told him.

'Oh! I see! I didn't know that you could trust what anybody else told you about your wife. I thought I, your wife, was the one you trusted most.'

'That's your opinion and you are entitled to it. My opinion is different,' he said haughtily.

'I see,' Pam replied.

'I can now understand why you want to go back to Kenya – very well-timed! When the truth is you have already arranged for an elopement with your lover!'

Pam nearly fainted. The statement had hurt her more than she could bear.

'Yes, my dear, faithful wife, I know the truth hurts, and naturally you are hurt.'

Pam, still gaping, said in an undertone, 'I would forgive you for anything else but this? No, Jim I will never, ever, ever forgive you for saying such a thing. It is unforgiveable, and all I can tell you for now is that I must go back home, I cannot live with you under the same roof after what you have said tonight. I must go home to my people, even if it means the end of our marriage. I must go.'

There was silence, so she continued, 'Anyway, you broke up our marriage a long time ago. We have just been hanging on to a spider's web, you can't pretend it's news to you.'

'Just what do you mean by saying that I broke up our marriage a long time ago?' he asked sharply.

'Yes, Jim, you destroyed our marriage long ago, and you know it. It's no use, Jim. You know you don't love me or want me anymore. We don't get on or understand each other. And now, with what you have just told me, I don't think I can take your insults anymore. One can only hear so much. It's no use you and I trying to hold together on sinking grounds – we have already sunk, Jim. I'd better go home and give you your freedom which, I think, you need and for which you are doing everything possible to get, short of driving me mad!'   ,

The animal in Jim struck and struck hard. Pam did not take record of what happened.

CHAPTER

12

◆ ◆ ◆ ◆

For two days, Pam lay half conscious in the hospital bed. She did not know where she was or what had happened. She spent most of the time in a state of delirium. When she fully woke up on the third day, she was told that there had been an accident; she had fallen down and as a result she had fractured her skull.

Brigadier Okonkwo had on hearing the news of Pam's sudden illness, rushed to the hospital to offer his personal sympathy to her. He was very concerned about her health and well-being; he consulted the doctor who was seeing her, privately and in total confidence, and was relieved to hear that she would be all right and that there was nothing to worry about. The x-rays had shown no serious head injury, only a superficial fracture and she was responding well to treatment.

On the other hand, Jim played his cards well and gave everybody the impression that he was a true Romeo. He took days off duty to be by Pam's bedside, pouring out his string of apologies and pleading for forgiveness. Pam just listened and said nothing. She was not impressed by what he said or did. She had a flash of what had happened in their house: the quarrel...

Jim saying that she was arranging to elope with George... the fatal slap... and now the hospital bed. She felt such a bitterness towards Jim that she gathered her strength and spoke to him.

'Jim, would you mind, please, leave me alone. Just go, and don't come back to see me... just...'

'Pam, darling, please don't send me away from you! I want to be with you ... to be near you. I don't want to go back to that haunted house. Honey, do please understand. Oh, good Lord! What a cad I have been! I would give anything, do anything, anything to undo all the wrongs I have done to you, Pam. I think I'm going crazy! Pam, please. I beg you... take me back! I'm like the prodigal son! I didn't realise what a fool I've been until now. Now I know what you Pam, my wife, means to me. I swear to the Almighty God that I will completely amend my ways! Just give me a chance, please Pam.'

There was silence as the nurse came to give Pam an injection. 'How are you feeling now, Mrs Mutisya?' the nurse asked innocently, not knowing that she'd hurt Pam by calling her 'Mrs Mutisya'.

'I'm not feeling too bad now. That pain I complained about this morning has gone.'

'You will get well soon,' the kind nurse said, as she picked up her tray of medicine and syringes and walked out, leaving husband and wife alone.

'Pam, please talk to me!'

'Talk to you about what? About the fatal slap you gave me?' she asked him bitterly.

'Pam, please forget about what happened and let's begin a new life... a new chapter for both of us. We are meant for each other, don't you understand?'

'Go and open that new chapter with Marie!'

Pam was bitter because she knew her Jim so well. He was a really dangerous pretender, who could laugh with you one minute and murder you the next. It had taken her this long to completely understand the kind of man she got married to. Whether the words that she'd uttered escaped Jim's hearing or not, Pam could not tell. He did not react at all to them; instead, he told her of the plans he had for her when she came out of the hospital.

Pam was in hospital for ten days. Under the doctor's instructions, she was to continue with complete bed-rest for at least another week or two. That gave Jim an opportunity to really play the devoted husband. He waited on her, this time, patiently.

Then one night, holding her against his chest, he said, 'Pam, I don't want to offend you by bringing back memories of an old story, but I do really want to apologise to you both for what I did that fateful day, and for what I said about you and George. I acted hastily and stupidly. I guess I was hurt by what had been said to me. Pam, that reliable source of information I talked about was the total opposite; I now know the whole story was supposed to provoke me. I must admit, the person succeeded to a point. Now I can assure you that I hold no grudge against Brigadier Okonkwo and I know you are, and have always been, faithful to me. You are my wife and you will remain so. Are you listening to me, Pam?'

Pam looked at him with a kind of look that held more of detest than love. She hated hearing what he was saying. 'What does it matter now?' she asked, letting out a bitter sob.

'Why, Pam? Why don't you want to believe me, to believe that I'm sorry, that I'm going to change, that I'm going to behave like your old Jim?'

'It's too late ... much too late, Jim, I just can't... '

'Oh, for Pete's sake, Pam!' He stammered the words out. 'Be reasonable! I'm telling you I was provoked... I was made to believe that... ' He stopped and then continued quietly, 'Does that mean you are not going to forgive me?'

'Take your choice but please leave me alone, Jim. Just be a man and leave me alone.'

'No, Pam. I cannot leave you alone, not until you say you have forgiven me and that you love me as you used to.'

'What does it matter now whether you were provoked or not? What's the use, Jim? You know very well that you and I will never be the way we used to be.'

Jim was getting slightly impatient about Pam's stubbornness and repeated refusal to acknowledge his apologies, but somehow he kept his patience. 'Listen, Pam please, I...'

'No use, Jim. And please, if you care for me and are really sorry for what you did, then arrange for my immediate flight home. That's the best thing you can do for me.'

That last statement had really scared Jim. 'Oh, no! No, Pam! You cannot go and leave me alone. You are all I have got in this world, Pam. I cannot let you go! No, no! Pam, look, I am sorry and I have told you so repeatedly. Please give me another chance to prove to you that I still love you.'

There was silence. Then Pam, with a great sigh, said, 'OK, Jim. Give me some time to think it over. But for now, please just leave me alone.'

'All right, Pam, if that's what you wish,' he said as he walked away from her.

The following day at work, Jim decided to swallow his pride as this was the right thing to do to save his marriage and face. Though with a lot of unwillingness in his heart, he walked into Brigadier Okonkwo's office. He always dreaded washing his dirty linen in public but he knew that his behaviour was not any news to the man he wanted to speak to. In fact, Jim had a feeling that the Brigadier already knew what was going on between him and Pam. There is no much harm; he convinced himself. He was certain that the Brigadier would be a better person to talk to about this matter.

'How are you, Sir?' Lieutenant-Colonel Mutisya greeted his senior officer.

'I'm fine, Jim. Take a seat,' Brigadier Okonkwo said, indicating an empty chair. 'How is everybody?' he continued.

'Well, everything is OK. Pam is a lot better now. She is still taking her drugs but will soon be up and about.'

Jim's apparent casualness annoyed George. He could have slapped the other man right on the face. *'This man has no sense of shame or decency! He's forgotten he's the cause of Pam's illness which nearly killed her, and he's such a hypocritical liar into the bargain that I could easily throw up!'* George thought bitterly, as he looked at Jim. His thoughts were interrupted by the telephone ringing. After a brief conversation, he stood up and put on his *Kofia*. He excused himself to Jim, with a promise to pass by his house later that evening, 'If only to have a glimpse of Pam,' he nearly said.

And so, that evening Brigadier Okonkwo called at Mutisya's house as he had promised earlier in the day. As the three had supper and drinks, Mutisya talked of taking more days off to take Pam for a short, holiday in one of the country's lodges. Of course, neither Pam nor Brigadier Okonkwo appreciated Jim's gesture as genuine.

Later, when George had gone and the two were alone, Pam spoke to Jim. 'Jim, I don't want to sound ungrateful, but I really don't want to go for that holiday you were talking about this evening. I would rather...'

'Why not, Pam? Why don't you want to rest in much quieter surroundings? I mean, away from the jeeps' noises and the constant hooting...'

Pam looked him straight in the eyes. 'Jim, you are the limit!' she said. 'You act as if you have completely forgotten all that has happened. The fact that you have regretted your actions and have chosen to be nice to me does not mean that I feel the same – nice and free with you; I don't feel that way at all, Jim, and you cannot expect me to act like the loving wife all of a sudden. It's not as easy as you think, Jim.'

There was silence. Pam couldn't believe what a shallow-minded, insensitive person her husband was. He seemed unable to comprehend how deeply Pam had been hurt by his behaviour. As far as Pam was concerned, the damage was permanent and their relationship now had very deep dents. Pam had come to terms with the situation and knew the only solution was for her to return to Kenya, alone.

'I see. You're just being stubborn, Pam. I suppose you want to spoil my reputation here and at home, and that's why you want to go. You are just impossible, Pam! Why do you want to ruin me? Why, Pam... why? Anyway, there is no question of you going home, don't forget we have struck a deal and...'

He did not finish the sentence before Pam interrupted him.

'I beg your pardon, Jim?' She was almost hysterical. 'Just what do you mean by saying we have "struck a deal"? You, you are impossible! You have no shame! You are unpardonable... you know very well you have ruined your own reputation. Don't think you can use me as a scapegoat!'

'Why shouldn't I use you? You are my wife, aren't you, Pam? And being my "wife",' he deliberately stressed the word "wife", 'we have struck a deal, we agreed to agree... that's what I mean by we...'

'Agreed to agree on what? Jim, you are the limit!' She turned to leave the room.

'Hey, hey...woman! Wait a minute...'

Pam stood still. No words came from her mouth. She was trembling with rage. After she calmed down, she finally found the words to talk to Jim. 'May I remind you, Jim, that you already killed a part of me by the way you have been treating me since my arrival here in Rhodesia. You have let yourself down, and let me down too. I really cannot understand how you expect me to be the same adoring and loving wife, behaving as if nothing has happened, when you are responsible, wholly responsible, for everything. You're like a creature from a different world, a world where mercy is unheard of!'

Through his selfish behaviour, Jim had hurt Pam far too much. His unfaithfulness, the way he had constantly bullied her, lied to her and tortured her both mentally and physically. All this had left a big wound in her heart, not even time could heal a wound this deep, yet her nemesis continued making pleas for forgiveness. In fact, his pleas only made Pam hate him all the more as she couldn't believe he was sincere.

After another spell of silence, Pam decided to make one last effort to persuade Jim to send her home, and with great difficulty she told him that there was only one thing she wanted him to do for her; if he really cared for her, and if there was to be any chance of a reconciliation, he must agree to send her home as soon as he could arrange it. She would even take a private flight if necessary.

'By going home, I will be able to compose myself and have some time to think it over, you know. Give me a break, Jim. Hopefully,' she ended with a helpless gesture, ' it will help both of us to think independently and maybe come to a decision, without being influenced by each other's emotions.'

There was more silence, a deadly hush. When Jim spoke, it was to coldly tell her that although he would consider her request, there were no flights to Nairobi for a month or two, and a private flight was out of the question.

Mutisya was as unpredictable with his love affairs as the Rhodesian weather. After the scene in Marie's apartment, he had sworn never ever to see her again. She was a bitch! A double-dealer, totally unworthy of his love. But, he was intrinsically a selfish man, and could not stand any woman he had had an affair with to be seen or associated with another man. Now, after his talk with his wife, which had been far from being successful, he saw things in a different light. If he allowed Pam to go home, which he eventually might be forced to, he would definitely need company, the company of a woman, of course, and a woman with whom he would not form ties or feel sorry to leave behind when his time to leave Rhodesia came. Such a woman, he concluded, could only be Marie; and with that conviction, he made up his mind to seek reconciliation with her.

The following day after lunch, Mutisya went to her apartment. He didn't have the slightest idea that she too was regretting for ever having invited another man to her apartment, and was longing to see Jim, to apologise. He had been the only man who had cared for her ever since her husband died. She could not compare Jim with any of the other men she had had affairs with. Her train of thoughts about Jim were interrupted by a knock on the door. She quickly rose to open it and there, in front of her was Jim! She could hardly believe her eyes.

'Jim! I'm so sorry for what happened! I promise it will never happen again. Please forgive me!' She didn't even wait for him to sit down. She couldn't control her tongue and found herself apologising profusely.

'Promise?' he said, looking her in the eyes.

'I promise, Jim. It won't happen again. I was just stupid, you see, just stupid! Please forgive me? Say you will, Jim … say you will!' She was now in his arms, and the two clung to each other like frightened children.

That evening when Mutisya got home, he was in a jovial mood. Marie had restored happiness to him by promising to love him alone. His manner was so jolly and convivial that Pam felt that something weird was happening; she could hardly believe what she was seeing or hearing from him. It was all very strange. They had their supper in a friendly and relaxed atmosphere, Jim doing the serving and humming romantic tunes as he went about the tasks.

'Tomorrow,' Jim began when they were in bed, 'I will be going for a recce, darling, and I might be late coming home. If I don't get back in time for supper, don't worry. We plan to go deep in the bush and we might be forced to camp overnight.'

'Do you want me to pack a few things for you, just in case?' she asked him, sleepily.

'Don't worry. I will only need my shaving kit, toothbrush, toothpaste, a comb and probably an extra shirt, which I can just put in my briefcase in the morning.'

'What time will you be leaving, Jim?'

'Not very early. Around seven or so. Why?'

'Oh, nothing really. I just want to know so that I can wake up and prepare your breakfast…'

'I don't really think I'll bother with any breakfast, darling, so don't wake up early.'

In good faith, Pam wished her husband a safe journey the following morning, and in return Jim kissed her on the cheek. 'Take care, Jim,' she told him as he got in the Land Rover.

'I will. You know I will, Pam,' he replied as he banged the door and drove off.

In her apartment, Marie was busy preparing her lover's breakfast and packing food and drinks for the picnic. It had all been arranged the previous day; the two were to go for a long drive away from everybody else, just the two of them. Mutisya was to fake a recce, for Pam's benefit.

No sooner had Jim got to her apartment than she came down the stairs to meet him. She had heard the Land Rover stop in front of her apartment. After their breakfast, he helped her put all the picnic stuff in the Land Rover. They drove away happily, without a care in the whole wide world. They had each other and that was all that mattered to them. Jim was in high spirits and in a reckless manner, and without realising how far his romantic emotions were carrying him, he had temporarily let go of the steering wheel to kiss his lover, completely unaware of the nearness of an on-coming vehicle.

'Jim, watch out!' Marie managed to scream. But her warning fell on deaf ears.

'Oh, come on, Marie! I've been driving for the last... ' Jim said no more. It was too late for him to defend his ego. There was a piercing screeching of brakes, a bang, the screaming and suddenly all was dead, dead quiet.

CHAPTER

13

♦ ♦ ♦ ♦

Evening came and Jim had not turned up. Pam was not surprised or worried; Jim had indicated that they would have to camp overnight if they didn't make it back. She relaxed on the couch, reading a novel which George had given her.

By sheer coincidence, Brigadier Okonkwo happened to be in the officers' mess that evening, and had decided on impulse to go and say 'Jambo' to the Mutisyas. He hadn't known that Jim was not in the house, and fully expected to find both Jim and Pam at home. His visit was much welcomed by Pam, who was just beginning to feel lonely and restless after concentrating for so long on reading a novel. After greeting George and welcoming him inside the house, she offered him a drink and poured some wine for herself too. They talked as they took their drinks, and eventually George asked Pam whether her husband had not come home yet, or whether he had come home and gone out again.

'No, he hasn't come home. In fact I don't think he will be coming home tonight; he went for a recce and told me that he might not be able to make it back tonight,' she confided in him.

'Oh, I see... ' George found himself saying, without really concentrating on his words. His memory was, in that split second, taken back to another day when he had seen Mutisya in the middle of nowhere, kissing another woman. He had told his wife the same thing. He wondered with bitterness who he might be kissing and whispering words of love to this time.

The evening was rapidly approaching and although Pam was not sure that Jim would come, she planned to prepare supper, just in case he turned up. She managed to persuade George to stay for supper. She quickly made a meal, and after eating they rested on the couch with their drinks.

As the evening wore on, George had all this time suppressed his longing to hold Pam in his arms so much that he could not control the urge any longer. He let go momentarily.

'Pam!' he said her name softly. 'I don't think I ought to see you again. You know I have no right to... I beg you to understand. I'm crazy about you, that's the problem, and you know it, Pam. I love you far too much, and there's nothing I can do to show you how I feel. I just want to take you in my arms and... and... ' He could not go on, the words stuck in his throat.

'George,' she said emotionally, 'I do understand.' She too stopped; she could not go on either. There was a moment of silence then, wiping away a falling tear from her eye, she continued, 'I think... I can try and understand, George, and...'

George could stand it no longer. He gathered Pam in his arms and kissed her hungrily and passionately. Pam completely surrendered her whole being to him. 'Pam, my darling Pam,' he whispered in her ear. 'We would be so happy together, you and I, if only fate had let us meet much earlier, before you got married. Pam, you are all that I want!'

'I know, George. I will always be grateful that I met you. You have completely changed my life; you have reminded me of being in love and of being loved. It is such a sweet feeling,

George ... your love all over my body! It is one of fate's cruel tricks that we've met each other too late. Soon, maybe very soon, we will be separated: you will go back to Nigeria and I to Kenya. We will be miles apart! Perhaps we will never meet again on this earth. Oh, George, I can't bear the thought of it!'

'Pam,' he spoke her name dreamily, 'don't let that worry you. We are human beings; we move and travel. We are not like mountains which can't move. Chances are that we shall meet... I mean it, on this very earth we shall meet, Pam. I will see to that. Remember, I told you I had been to your lovely country, Kenya? I will come again, Pam, for your sake,' he assured her.

When George left Pam that night, she was feeling on top of the world. She and Jim had parted amicably that morning, and George had dropped in unexpectedly. She felt drunk with happiness, and when she went to bed, she slept like a log until the following morning.

Pam did not wake up until eleven o'clock the following morning. After having a shower, she prepared a hearty breakfast for herself. It was while she was having her breakfast that somebody knocked at her door. She rose to open it, expecting to see her husband but her jovial mood was instantly reduced to one of terrible fear on seeing an army ambulance waiting outside her house. Her heart stopped beating momentarily, a fearful, cold chill ran down her spine and suddenly, immense fear gripped her. Her instincts seemed to tell her that something was wrong, very wrong... but what? *'What could be wrong?'* She wondered.

Standing in front of her were Major Njoroge, his wife Kate, and another Kenyan officer whom Pam knew to be Captain Oyugi. Much as Kate tried to hide her grief, Pam was quick to notice that Kate had been crying.

'Kate!' Her voice was a hoarse whisper. 'Kate, what's the matter? What's wrong?' Her whole body was now shaking uncontrollably.

'Pam,' Major Njoroge cleared his throat. 'Pam, it's going to be all right. I'm sorry to have to tell you that there has been an accident, and … ' Words failed Njoroge too. He just could not go on. He did not know how to tell Pam the dreadful news.

'No! No! Njoroge! Jim!' Pam screamed, hysterically. 'Tell me the truth – Jim is dead… isn't he? Isn't he? Oh, tell me, is he?' She began to weep.

'Pam, calm down please! You see, we don't know yet – we hope not. It was just a message that came to us. All we know is that he was taken to hospital and his condition is not very good. They'll let us know as soon as there's any news.'

'I want to go to him. Please take me to Jim! Oh, Kate… oh,'she cried.

'Of course, Pam. I will make arrangements for you to be taken to the hospital,' Njoroge promised.

By lunchtime the house was full of people enquiring about her husband's condition. Among the first to come was Brigadier Okonkwo. At that time, no official report about the accident had been received. The only available information was that his vehicle had been involved in a head-on collision with a truck. Mutisya had suffered a head injury and was in a critical condition, while his female passenger, whose name had been withheld till the next of kin were informed, had died instantly.

Pam was totally confused and in a state of shock. She kept on hoping that it was all a terrible nightmare and that she would wake up and find there hadn't been an accident at all. Jim would be coming home anytime. But with Kate crying softly by her side, trying to tell her to take courage and that all would be well and that Jim would pull through, made her realise that it was not a dream.

'Perhaps Jim will never come back to this house again. Poor Jim. Only yesterday we seemed to be good friends. He had even kissed me goodbye, not knowing that perhaps he would never kiss me again,' Pam reflected.

Jim was unconscious for four days. When he regained his consciousness, he was totally confused and could not remember anything, not even Pam, who had been constantly by his side. However, the doctor treating him assured Pam that Jim had a fifty-fifty chance of regaining his full memory in time. Operation after operation was performed on Jim, some very delicate and requiring extreme care, and others not so delicate. The most crucial ones were on his skull, to ascertain the extent of brain damage, and the removal of one of his kidneys, which had been damaged beyond repair.

Although his progress was slow, it was nevertheless encouraging. He was responding well to the treatment and after four weeks in the hospital's Intensive Care Unit, he was transferred to a small, private room. He was then officially confirmed as being off the danger list.

Jim was in the hospital bed for three months before he was discharged. Despite being very weak, he was well and almost completely recovered. He had also regained his memory fully. However, one of his legs had been badly fractured and a piece of metal had been inserted between the bones. This made him limp and he had to learn to walk with the help of a metallic walking aid. For this reason, the doctors had recommended that Jim should only do light duties. There was no question of Jim carrying on his old job, sometimes travelling for long distances in a country, where there were no proper roads. This condition meant the end of his stay in Rhodesia.

Pam was extremely thankful to the doctors and all those who had worked so hard and tirelessly round the clock to save her husband's life. Apart from the hospital staff, Pam was particularly grateful to Major Njoroge, Kate and Brigadier Okonkwo, all of whom never ceased to comfort her. Kate literally became a mother to Pam, and Pam responded as a daughter would to her mother. They had become part of the family and Pam was happy that Jim had totally accepted Brigadier Okonkwo as a true and genuine friend, and did not feel resentful towards him anymore. Jim had sincerely apologised to him and they had toasted to that. As for Pam, only actions and time would tell whether Jim had really reformed for good.

Three weeks after his discharge from the hospital, Jim and Pam returned to Kenya. It had been sad for Jim to leave his many friends behind, especially Brigadier Okonkwo, whom he had come to love and had nicknamed 'Big Brother'. On the evening of their departure, Jim and Pam had asked a few people to their married quarters for dinner and drinks. They used the occasion to thank them all and to wish them a safe and happy stay. Jim was in particularly high spirits, and both he and Pam were looking forward to their new life with optimism.

As a last gesture of gratitude to Brigadier Okonkwo, Jim invited him to come to Kenya as his personal guest when time allowed. 'It does not matter when, it may be years before you can come, Sir, but I want you to know that you will always be welcome as my guest,' Jim told him.

All their relatives and friends were at the Jomo Kenyatta International Airport to meet Jim and Pam. They were aware that Jim had had an accident, but it was never fully explained; the only information they ever received was on his progress and his quick recovery. No one, even his office, knew how the accident had occurred and so it was assumed that it must have been caused by a tyre burst.

A few weeks after their arrival, Jim resumed his duties but he was now based at the Headquarters in Nairobi so that he could get medical treatment for his leg at the Forces' Memorial Hospital. Pam, too, got a job at the bank with her old employer. Being back home meant a lot for Pam. She was now close to her mother and all those whom she loved. She was also particularly happy for Jim, for like her, he had put the past behind him and they had begun a new chapter in their lives. Their life was now a happy marriage, and they both hoped that they would get a child. True to their prayers, they got a baby girl, whom they called Joy Mueni. She was called Joy because, they said, 'She has been given to us to add more happiness to us. She is joy itself to us!'

Joy's arrival was wonderful news and was shared with their family, friends and relatives who went to the *Kukwata Mwana* ceremony. They brought gifts to the new baby. In addition to all others, one special person sent his gift all the way from Nigeria – Brigadier George Okonkwo. The peace-keeping forces had been withdrawn a few months after Jim and Pam had left Rhodesia because the fighting groups had agreed on a cease-fire in order to pave way for their country's independence.

Jim, now a totally reformed character, was very happily settled with his wife, Pam and their little daughter, Joy. Within two years after his return to Kenya, Jim was promoted to full Colonel and posted to France as Kenya's Military Adviser. This was a tremendous opportunity, and this news was well received by Pam. Pam had always wanted to learn French but had never had the opportunity. Now that Jim had been posted to France itself, she could not see the posting as anything else but an opportunity for her to pursue her dream.

Two months after their arrival in France, Jim and Pam enrolled for French classes. Little Joy went to nursery, where she too learnt to speak French. Even after this posting abroad, one person that Jim and Pam did not forget to get in touch with was Brigadier George Okonkwo. They wrote to him and informed him of Jim's promotion and subsequent posting to France. When he replied, he told Jim and Pam that he too had been promoted, to the rank of Major-General. They were thrilled to hear the good news. They sent him a congratulatory card!

Life in France was full of happiness for the Mutisyas; Jim loved his wife every hour of the day.

'Miracles do still happen,' Jim told Pam one evening, as they had dinner in one of the most exclusive hotels in France. 'I don't intend to open old wounds, Pam, but God knows, I'm so happy I married you, Pam! I'm sure no other woman would have put up with what you have.' He paused and then went on, 'God loves us, Pam and I will do everything I can to make you and Joy the happiest human beings on this earth! I know, with His help, I will!'

'I know you will, Jim. You have already made us happy more than you know. I'm glad too that I married you, Jim,' Pam replied, with such charm that Jim could not help but kiss her hand.

Despite all that Pam had been through, she still loved Jim. With time, she had grown to forgive and forget the past, and she was more determined than ever to help Jim make their marriage a very happy one. So far, she had succeeded in achieving this wish.

Jim and Pam had been in France for three years already when their stay was extended for three more years. This news was received with mixed feelings by both Jim and Pam. They had hoped to return to Kenya after the first three-year stint, which was the normal posting for military advisers abroad. After the extension, Jim and Pam agreed that Pam should come home ahead and look for a good property to buy in Nairobi. They had saved some money and it was time they invested it.

Pam landed in Nairobi and proceeded straight to Kangundo, her in-laws' home. As a true African woman, she stayed with her and Mutisya's relatives for a few days before going to see her mother. When she returned to Nairobi where she stayed with the Njoroges. Kate was overjoyed to have her good friend Pam as her guest, and often accompanied her to see some of the property advisers.

After two weeks of going round viewing properties, Pam finally settled for one in Karen, a house standing on a ten-acre plot. Jim had every confidence in his wife, and had given her the authority to conduct the sale. She succeeded in negotiating the price of the property with the owner, and immediately sent some photographs of the property to Jim. He wrote straight back to her after receiving it, indicating he was quite impressed with her choice.

'I always knew you would make a better choice than I would, Pam. You have my full support and blessing to go right ahead with the deal,' he concluded his letter to her.

Within a few weeks, a four-year lease agreement had been signed between Pam and the company which was leasing the property. Pam returned to France. She was glad to be back with Jim and Joy, who had now grown to a sweet little girl. Two years before they left for Kenya, Jim and Pam received a double blessing: Jim had been promoted further to the rank of Brigadier, and Pam gave birth to twin boys – Kimeu and Mutiso – later christened Philip and Michael respectively. The twins brought more happiness to them. The news of the twins' arrival was received by their parents with great happiness and was seen as a true blessing. Giving birth to twins was no longer taken as a curse, as in the olden days, when the babies would be killed and the mother branded a witch.

Kept busy by the twins, Pam did not realise how fast weeks turned to months, and months to years. Their remaining two years' stay was over and they began packing to come home.

'I really will miss this place, but I'm so happy to be going home after all this time. There is no better place than home!' she told Jim as they packed.

In Nairobi, Jim took an official residence while he waited for his tenant's lease to expire. As they both agreed, Pam did not seek any employment, but set up a French–English translation bureau. With this in mind, they had already bought all the necessary equipment in France and shipped them over a few weeks before their departure. Pam also had to do some farming on their farm and would keep some dairy cattle when they moved in. Life once more seemed to be falling into place after the upheaval of the move from France. Pam, especially, was excited about her new translation venture.

His leave over, Jim too resumed his duties in very high spirits after all the relaxation. It had been a long time since he had worked among his fellow officers, some of whom had been promoted to senior posts. Now, himself a very senior officer, he was in charge of a newly set up Training College for the Armed Forces.

It was mid July, a very cold month in Kenya – very chilly indeed. During that particular year, the weather was terribly cold, and to chase the cold away, Jim jogged most evenings after work. Sometimes, he was joined by Pam. As it had become his habit, Jim came home from work one evening, had his cup of tea and then changed into his jogging suit. He then went out for his jog along the road. Before he could go very far from his house, he suddenly felt a sharp pain in his chest and experienced difficulty in breathing. He had barely run; at that point he was only walking and he could not understand why he had got a pain and difficulty in breathing. He could not continued and decided to go back home. He took a hot bath, hoping that he would feel better and warmer, but he only seemed to feel worse.

This got Pam so worried. She took him to a hospital, where he was admitted immediately. The diagnosis revealed that he was suffering from very acute pneumonia and required close medical attention. The doctor assured Pam that her husband would be all right, and told her to go home and come back the following morning. Jim, too, assured Pam that he was not feeling so bad and promised that he would see her the next day. He urged her to go home and get some sleep. It was with such confident assurances that Pam left the hospital and went home.

Continuous ringing of the phone by her bedside woke Pam up. It startled her from a dream which instinct told her was not a good dream at all. Pam, with hands trembling not because of cold but from her inner fear, answered it.

'Mrs Mutisya?' the male voice at the other end asked softly. 'Sorry to have woken you up at this hour of the night, but it is important that you come to the hospital immediately.'

'It's my husband Doctor, isn't it? How is he? Please tell me!' Pam gasped, she felt so breathless with fear.

'Nothing serious, but your presence is required here, Mrs Mutisya,' the doctor told her as calmly as he could.

Even as the doctor spoke to her, she detected some reservation in his voice and smelt danger. 'I'll be there right away, Doctor.'

As she drove, Pam was in a delirium; she kept on thinking that she was still dreaming, that she was not really driving at all – until she entered the hospital. She found herself running along the corridor until she reached the room where Jim had been admitted. The night duty nurse was in time to intercept her just before she opened the door to Jim's room. As soon as Pam saw the doctor's face, she knew the worst had happened; she didn't need to be told – the sad message was written on the doctor's face, much as he tried to professionally hide the truth.

'I'm sorry, Mrs Mutisya,' the doctor began, but he didn't get any further. Pam fainted. It took several minutes before she regained consciousness. When she did come to, she found herself surrounded by nurses.

'Where am I? What happened?' she enquired faintly.

'You are in hospital, Mrs Mutisya,' one of the nurses answered gently.

'Hospital! What am I doing in hospital?'

'You fainted, Mrs Mutisya, but you are all right now.'

Then gradually Pam came to her full senses. She tried to remember what had happened. She remembered the doctor's telephone call, the drive to the hospital and... 'Oh God!' she suddenly wailed, and wept uncontrollably. 'Is it true, Doctor ... true that my husband is? Oh, Doctor, please tell me it is not true! That it is all a dream, a nightmare! Oh, please, somebody tell me... take me to Jim! Take me to him.'

'Please lie down, Pam.'

'Oh, Kate! Kate... Kate... what are they telling me? That Jim is dead? Tell them Kate! Tell them... ' Pam became even more hysterical on seeing Kate and her husband. Obviously, they had been informed of Jim's death immediately.

The doctor had to sedate Pam. Kate and Njoroge sat with her for several hours. By mid-morning, Pam was discharged and Kate and Njoroge took her home.

The news of Jim's sudden death spread like bush fire. The house was full of mourners from Kangundo and Nairobi by that evening. Pam had asked Njoroge to send a telegram to Major-General Okonkwo, informing him of the sad news. George was very upset and saddened, and although due to official duty he could not make it to the funeral, he wrote to Pam and expressed his sympathies. He promised to come and see her when time allowed.

Brigadier Jim Mutisya was buried with full military honours a week after his death at his Kangundo home. Pam and the children stayed behind after the funeral for a few weeks before going back to Nairobi to resume her farming. Nothing was quite the same without her husband, Jim, who for many years had been a perfect, loving husband and father. She loved him. Now that he had left her and gone beyond her reach, she did not know what to do. At first, life had seemed hopeless, not even worth living, but then somewhere in the depths of her mind, she remembered something Jim had once written when he'd wanted her to go to Rhodesia, 'Pam, you are now my wife, a soldier's wife, and you must be prepared for changes and cope with them.'

'But, Oh God,' she thought, *'this is too much of a change for me to cope with! Oh Jim! Why ... why did you go and leave me? I could have coped with any other changes, but this... this...,* ' she wept bitterly.

CHAPTER
14

◆ ◆ ◆ ◆

It took Pam several months to emerge from her lonely shell and decide that life must go on. She realised that Jim was not on safari, after which he would come back to her. She had to be the soldier's wife, be brave, sensible and cope with the change. She was on her own now, both mother and father for Mueni, Kimeu and Mutiso who by now were growing children in school. They were fully aware of what had happened–their father was no more.

Pam was very lucky because, unlike many other widows who forfeited their late husbands' properties to their in-laws, Jim's family loved her very much and could only think of helping her to cope with life without Jim, without also taking away what she and Jim owned. If Pam felt lonely, it was only when she went to bed and found herself alone in the bedroom. During most days, she was kept busy on the *shamba*, looking after her dairy cattle, chicken, and flower beds. She and Jim had just begun to grow flowers and French beans for the export market. In time, Pam resigned her post at the bureau and decided to go into farming full time.

Several years passed by, and Pam gradually grew used to life without Jim, physically, but spiritually she always consulted him on whatever decision she had to make. The many friends they had made together were always on hand to help her. However, the one whom she treasured most was Major-General Okonkwo. He never stopped writing to her and she always looked forward to reading his comforting letters. The only thing that never failed to amaze her was that George had not yet got married, and he avoided the issue when, in one of her letters to him, Pam had suggested to him that when he married he might come to Kenya for his honeymoon. She said she would love to have him and his wife as her guests.

The Njoroges were another source of constant support and comfort for Pam and they often took her for dinner and to parties, especially when such parties were in the officers' mess. She was still one of them – a fact that made her feel even more comforted. She could get assistance from any of the armed forces personnel, whenever she needed it.

'That,' Pam thought, 'is one of the most coveted traditions within the armed forces; they still make you feel you are one of them, that you belong to them even after your husband's death. Thank God that Jim chose to join such a noble career!'

After a hard day's work, Pam was having her dinner with the Njoroges in her house when the 'Voice of Kenya' was broadcasting the nine o'clock news. Usually the headlines of the local news were read first, and then the international news headlines before the full reports were read out. However, the newscaster read out an international headline first. That gave Pam and the Njoroges a sudden shock.

'News Flash! It has been learnt from Lagos that the Nigerian Government has been overthrown in a bloody coup... '

'Oh, my God!' was all they could say. The news was a big shock to each of them, as they thought of their good friend, George. Pam knew George's telephone number, but she felt it was no use trying to put a call through. Communication with the rest of the world would have been the first thing to be cut off by the coup plotters. She had to be contented with what was broadcast on television and reported in the dailies. It was such a mental torture for Pam; more so because she didn't even know whether he was alive or dead.

Weeks turned to months and still Pam had not heard anything from George. She began to fear that George must have either been killed or detained. 'Detained might be better, because at least he will probably come out, one day. But what if he was killed... *'No, no!'* She did not want to think about it and just hoped and prayed that all was well with George.

It was a chilly day in June and Pam would have loved to stay indoors by the fireside, but she remembered she had a dentist's appointment in town; she must have this troublesome tooth filled otherwise she would have another sleepless night!

After leaving the dentist's clinic, Pam decided to check whether there was any post in her mail box. She found a few bills, some cheques in payment for the chicken and milk deliveries to various places and then, an airmail which was posted from Britain!

'A letter from Britain?' Pam nearly asked the question aloud. *'But who could have... I don't know anybody in Britain!'* She tore open the letter and there it was – George's name and address in Britain! Breathlessly, she read the letter through without digesting any of its contents. Her mind was spinning around, her eyes were moist with tears of happiness and gratitude that George was alive. Even the pain from the dentist's drilling and filling her tooth was washed away by the happiness she felt. She was so overjoyed that she could cry and shout aloud.

'After what happened at home, I was very lucky to get away before things worsened. I would have been a victim, that's certain, since I was not on the plotters' side – but God is Great! He helped me in good time and I managed to get away from it all. I'm all right now, and I have got a good job and have settled down here in Britain. My family at home is well and we communicate somehow,' he wrote.

After reading that first paragraph and reassuring herself that George was all right, Pam walked to her car and read the rest of the letter while sitting in the car. The next paragraph nearly left her breathless. 'Pam, if all goes well, I plan to spend my next summer holidays in your beautiful country, Kenya. I hope I will not be asking you for too much if I request that you make hotel bookings for me. I would very much appreciate it, and will send you more details when the time comes.'

'George coming for his holidays here in Kenya! That will be wonderful!' Kate said, when Pam told her of the letter.

'Oh, Kate, I'm so glad that he is safe, if nothing else...,' Pam told her friend.

Pam was a good letter–writer, as was George, and they communicated every now and then, each looking forward to their next meeting. Knowing that if Jim was alive, he would agree – or rather insist – that George stayed with them in their house, Pam decided to put George up in her guest-wing rather than book him in a hotel. Having decided this, she told her children now big and in high school, of George's visit. Although the children had not actually met him, they had seen his photograph taken with their late father in Rhodesia, and were eager to meet him.

The days passed very quickly and soon there was only a week to go before George's arrival. George's flight touched down at Jomo Kenyatta International Airport at 0900 hours on a bright morning. Pam had arrived there half an hour earlier to pick him up. As the passengers lined up at the exit for the customs check, Pam spotted George and waved at him. He waved back, with a broad smile. *'He has not changed much... only his hair's a little thinner,'* she reflected. As soon as George was cleared by customs, he walked straight over to Pam. He could not help but hug her, and Pam would not have wished it otherwise. For a moment they both seemed to think of Jim, and Pam couldn't help a tear falling down. It was a happy and emotional reunion.

'I'm so sorry for all that you have been through, Pam,' George spoke at last.

'Thanks, George. It was one of those things that can't be stopped. I'm sorry too for what happened in your country, but I'm glad you managed to steer away from trouble in good time.'

'Well, Pam, that's politics and love of power for you.'

As they drove through Nairobi, George assumed Pam was taking him to a hotel. Pam hadn't told him that she had not actually booked a hotel room, but instead had prepared a guest wing for him. It was, therefore, a big surprise to George when Pam told him of the arrangements.

'Oh, Pam! You shouldn't have! Oh, I don't know what to say!

Did you really do all this for me?' George ran short of words to express his gratitude to Pam.

'You don't have to thank me, George. I'm sure Jim would have done the same for you, and so I did just what he would have done. Of course, if you really want I could still make arrangements for you to move in a hotel..., ' she teased.

'Oh, Pam, you don't know what this means to me ... I'm so happy and I really appreciate your offer. I haven't the slightest wish to move into a hotel!'

During the first few weeks of his stay, George toured most of the National Game Parks – Pam had arranged all that with a city touring company. Then, accompanied by Pam, he went down to the coast for a two–week holiday. Pam had had many friends, some of whom had wanted to marry her, but she always turned their proposals down. She felt she could never substitute Jim with anyone else and if she ever did, one thing was for sure, she could never marry a civilian man. That was out of the question; she could not live with a civilian husband, in the same house, never! If she was ever to think of marrying again, therefore, it must be to a man in the armed forces.

Down at the coast, Pam and George stayed in a five star hotel, where they enjoyed each other's company to the fullest. It was there one night, after they had had dinner and both were relaxing in a quiet corner of the lounge with their drinks that George poured out his heart to Pam. He had loved her ever since he'd first met her that afternoon and had taken her for a ride in Rhodesia, though now Zimbabwe.

'That afternoon I saw myself talking with Janet, my Janet, and I would have done anything on this earth to win your love... but then you were somebody else's wife. Pam, dear, I could not and I still do not understand how two people could be so alike, yet so far away from one another – one dead and another living. It completely defeated me and I still don't understand it. I almost believed in reincarnation when I saw you there! Nevertheless, there you were... unknowing and quite unaware of the effect you had on me!' George told Pam. Before she knew it, tears were rolling down her cheeks uncontrollably. George had reminded her of her days in Rhodesia, and of her dead husband.

'Pam, what's the matter?' George asked with great concern. 'Oh, George!' was all that she managed to say before she broke down. George moved closer to her, gave her his handkerchief and held her round the waist while he left her to cry out her heart on his shoulder. He knew that by letting her crying she would feel better; crying is the most natural way of releasing one's inner tensions. When she had cried her memories out, she looked up at George and smiled apologetically.

'Are you all right now, Pam?' he asked her gently.

'Yes, George, I guess I'm OK. I'm sorry. I didn't mean to break down like this!'

'That's, all right, Pam. I think you need a drink now,' he said, as he beckoned a passing waiter. 'A Double Brandy and ginger-ale and a cold White-Cap for me, please.'

It was Pam who brought up the subject of Rhodesia again as they had their drinks. She recounted her ups and downs while she was there, only this time she was not bitter about it; for now she just felt sorry that Jim was no longer with her. She had totally forgiven all the wrongs that Jim had done to her by dismissing them as young people's blood activities!

'Pam, I want you to be happy. I want to be the man to give you that happiness if you'll give me the chance. Pam, I want to be the one who will take your heart! I want to steal it and take it with me to the end of the world, where nobody knows us!'

'Oh, George... you are so romantic. You make me feel eighteen.'

'You are much younger than you think, Pam. You are so sweet and beautiful; you grow younger and more beautiful every day that passes!'

'George... I... I don't know what to say to you. You are so good to me. I don't know if I can do without you now, George...' She hesitated, then could hold back the words no longer, 'I love you George, and I know you are the only person who can make me happy.'

George and Pam eventually came back to Nairobi with news that all who knew Pam looked forward to. The knot that had been hanging loose long before Mutisya's death had to be tied, to be tied with a foreigner whose fiancée had reincarnated in Pam.

Printed in the United States
By Bookmasters